0

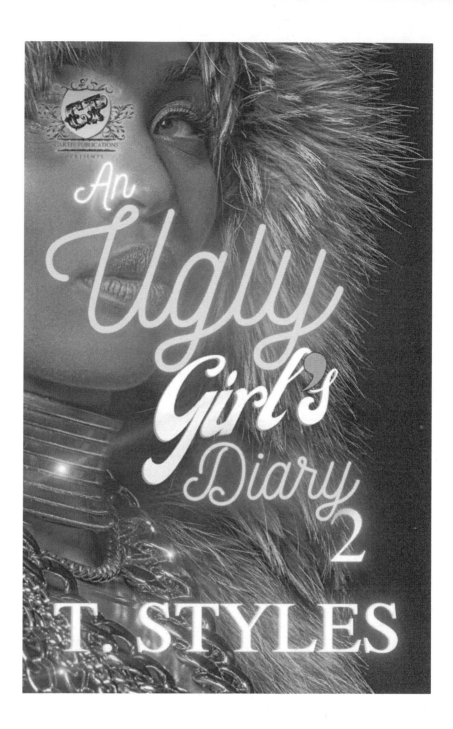

An Ugly Girl's Diary 2

T. STYLES

ARE YOU ON OUR EMAIL LIST?

SIGN UP ON OUR WEBSITE

www.thecartelpublications.com

3

4

WWW.THECARTELPUBLICATIONS.COM

AN UGLY GIRL'S DIARY

2

By

T. STYLES

Library of Congress Control Number:
2022914651

ISBN 10: 1948373890

ISBN 13: 978-1948373890

Cover Design: BOOK SLUT CHICK

First Edition

Printed in the United States of America

What Up Famo,

I hope and pray this love note finds y'all well. We made it through another holiday season and are heading into Spring! I can't believe it, but I am looking forward to it.

We have some great things in store for you family, starting with this book, *An Ugly Girl's Diary 2,* as well as gearing up to shoot our 9th film project, *A Hustler's Son – **The Movie**.*

This one is extra special because it was the book that got T. Styles her Triple Crown Publications deal and kicked off her career. So be on the lookout for it in the coming months. As well as all our other movie projects:

I'm Home; Mother Monster (Raunchy); Pitbulls in A Skirt; Bmore Chicks 1 & 2; It'll Cost You; and *The Worst of Us 1 & 2.* All are currently streaming on **TUBI**, except for The Worst of Us, which will be added on there soon, hopefully.

Now, go on ahead and get yourself whatever you like to eat, smoke or drink while you read and enjoy because this one is gonna take you on a crazy ride!

With that being said, keeping in line with tradition, we want to give respect to a vet, new trailblazer paving the way or pay homage to a favorite. In this novel, we would like to recognize:

David Jolicoeur, aka Trugoy the Dove

David "Trugoy The Dove" Jolicoeur was a member of the classic and legendary group, **De La Soul**. Man, I can't tell you how many times back in the early 90's their music took me away from anything I was dealing with in my life in the moment. I was saddened to hear of Trugoy's passing and I am praying for his soul, and his family. I'm grateful to him and De La Soul for their contribution to Hip-Hop and my young adult life.

Aight, my loves, catch you later...Enjoy!
Charisse "C. Wash" Washington
Vice President
The Cartel Publications
www.thecartelpublications.com

#ANUGLYGIRLSDIARY2

This Is Dedicated To The Reticent

The light is not always on you...
It shines on others too...

CHAPTER ONE
PRETTY PIRATE

Winter hit the streets hard as fuck this time around.

An icy breeze whipped around twenty-eight-year-old Valentina Cash's cocaine white Tesla as she drove slowly down the wet road. Unraked leaves danced like confetti at Mardi gras as she gripped the steering wheel with all her might. To keep the hawk out, she wore her golden gray wolf fur coat, with the hood on which concealed her bone-straight black hair. It also made it difficult to see peripherally but it was more about "the look" than it was "looking" at her surroundings.

Her best friend and future sister-in-law, Larisa Hart, sat in her passenger seat. A pair of black binoculars with night vision were pressed against her eye sockets, as she peered at every porch that Valentina drove by.

Larisa was fine as fuck and she knew it too.

Tall and confident, her skin was a rich, dark brown, which made her stand out even more, considering she wore a platinum blonde boy cut and had high cheekbones as round as small juicy peaches. Her lips, a natural hot pink and her ass stacked like it had been created by Dr. Miami himself.

And yet with all that beauty, they were fucking thieves.

"You see the house yet?" Valentina asked, wiping her hair out of her face, as it slammed into the fur of her coat. "'Cause we should have seen it by now."

She put the binoculars down slowly and glared. "Look, you gonna stop pressing me the fuck out." Her voice was low. "I'm doing the best I can."

The wind rushed harder, causing Valentina, a Baltimore native, to get nervous.

But there was reason to be afraid.

When she was a child her grandmother's house went up in a tornado as she sat in a tow truck to prevent flying away. To this day she had never seen her mother and father, essentially losing everything she loved.

"Got one." Larisa muttered while snapping on a piece of gum.

"Uh...you know you don't have to whisper right?"

"Oh...yeah." She scratched her low-cut blonde hair.

"Now where is it exactly? Is that the package on your list?"

"Nah...I just spotted something else."

"I don't feel like being out here all night. Let's just stick to picking up the boxes we know got product. You can–."

"If we see one, we take it, remember?" Larisa pointed across the way at a brick house with several packages sitting on the step. "So slow down and let's get this money."

"I guess so," Valentina observed the boxes glowing a soft brown under the night lamp. "Make it quick though. We have some place else to be." Valentina continued.

"We got time," Larisa said. "Trust me." Then she shoved her friend's hood down, so she could see her hazel eyes. "We gonna be good."

Valentina nodded. "Okay, you ready to go get it?"

She frowned. "Me?"

"Larisa, don't play. I got the last four."

"First of all you a fucking liar. You got one of the last four. I got the other ones while you were listening to that podcast."

"It's not *a* podcast it's-."

"The only podcast," Larisa mimicked sarcastically, repeating something Valentina said constantly.

"Exactly, and I didn't get a chance to finish because-."

"Are you gonna get the bitch or not, Valentina? Let's not forget I'm the one who gets the addresses from work. I could lose my job for this shit."

"Exactly, so why fuck with stuff not on the list?"

"Because I need the money. I gotta move out of that place."

"You 'bout to be married so–."

"You know it's best to have your own."

Valentina took a deep breath and looked out her window. The trees rocked back and forth like green monsters with tiny brown branch hands ready to snatch her soul. Trekking the weather when it was like this wasn't her bag. "I...I'll pay you more."

Larisa squinted her eyes. "How much more?"

"Does it fucking matter? I mean you acting broke by wanting to go get the shit, so you might as well state your fucking price."

"I'ma let you be mean because, well to be honest I'm used to it at this point." She paused. "But this soft shit making my pussy itch."

"Well you betta go get that checked before you give it to my brother."

"Bitch, what you gonna do?" Larisa snapped.

The wind rocked the car, rattling Valentina's nerves even more. "Look, I'm not the one stuck in a one-bedroom apartment, working a bullshit job and fucking for money on the side." She leaned closer. "You, Miss Broke Bitch." She pointed at herself with a gold crystal nail. "Not me."

"I *used* to fuck for money on the side." Larisa looked down and out the window at the house which had the package and back at Valentina. "Okay...I'm going 'cause I'm sick of your fucking mouth." Larisa slammed the hoodie from her royal blue jacket over her head and pushed the door open.

Valentina remained still, the engine purring quietly as she waited for her to complete their mission.

But Larisa moved panther like. And although the wind knocked off her hood as she approached the large house, she prowled with purpose and determination in the darkness.

Watching her was always a show which caused Valentina's heart to race with a mix of excitement and nervousness as she kept an eye out for any signs of danger.

And then Valentina saw what had become her enemy in her quest for the paper.

An HD camera.

Sure most people had cameras on their homes these days. But most of them were grainy and would fail in court. But this camera hung from the light pole, and she was certain the footage may have been as clear as a FL diamond.

"Fuck...fuck....fuck."

Did Larisa see the camera too? If she did, she didn't appear to be worried as she reached down and grabbed the stacked package tower and rushed toward the car.

Larisa was almost in the clear.

And then the lights from the house clicked on and the red curtain in the large front window pushed to the side, revealing an older white man with thick dark brown glasses, and angry eyes peeking through.

Packages being left at night was sometimes an indicator that folks weren't home. *So why was his ass in the house?* She thought. *Fuck he leave his shit out on the step for anyway?*

Valentina's stomach churned as the curtain closed and the front door flew open. Packages in hand, Larisa was almost in the car when, "Come back here!" The man yelled, tight fists swinging in the air. "That's mine!"

She didn't stop.

Just continued to dip and before long she was at the Tesla.

Yanking the door open, she tossed the packages in the backseat with the rest they collected for the evening and slammed the door. Then she opened the front door and slipped into the seat.

But before she could close it, he grabbed her by the hood. "You not going nowhere, bitch!"

"Get off me!" She yelled, swinging like she was in the right and had paid for them in full. "Let me go!"

"Well give me back my shit!" He hollered, as he began to fight her like a man. Bringing a tight fist down on her left cheek which made her ear inflamed.

Valentina felt gut punched.

The thing was this, if she didn't help, her friend would be in trouble. But if she was caught, she could get locked up and the safe lifestyle she built would be in vain. And trust, there was no place she feared more than prison.

Check the history...

One of her aunts was murdered in prison by her cellmate.

One of her friends went to prison for fighting and came out blind.

And finally, Larisa's ex-boyfriend went to prison and to the day no one knew where he was.

Going to jail was out of the question but still, she had to help Larisa.

Pushing the door open, Valentina was immediately smacked in the cheeks with a frigate wind so strong it wrapped her hair around her face. Instead of rising to the occasion, suddenly Valentina was trapped in fear once again.

Unable to move.

Unable to help.

Unable to breathe.

Visions of a tornado ruining her life flashed in her mind.

"Girl, do something!" Larisa screamed as she continued to fight with the man. Then she directed her attention toward him because he was kicking her ass. "Get off...get...off...me!"

"Look at all them packages you have in that fucking car!" The man yelled as he tried to pull her to the street. Her knees slammed into the concrete and her face was directly next to his crotch. "The cops are gonna love your thick black ass. You won't—."

His statement was cut short when Larisa bit down on his penis as hard as a jackhammer. She went past skin, cartilage and deeper to the soft bloody, gushy center.

"Arrrggghhhhhhh....you bit me!! You fucking bit me!" This caused him to completely release the hold he had on her as he tended to his dick. Falling on the grass, he placed both hands between his legs to save what was left. "I can't believe you bit me, bitch! I can't believe you bit me!"

"Well believe it, white nigga!"

A little delirious due to the blows, she wiggled back into the passenger seat and closed and locked the door. But what about Valentina, who was standing alongside the car unable to move.

"Bitch, get in! What you doing?"

Still in complete agony, the man placed one hand on Larisa's door handle as he struggled to rise.

22

"Get in and close the fucking door! Friday the 13th gonna kill our ass!"

Valentina remained stuck until Larisa reached over, yanked her by the fur and pulled her inside.

"Wake the fuck up!"

The man was now on his feet as he moved furiously toward the back, on his way to the driver's side.

"Go! Now!"

Valentina blinked a few times, back into reality. Realizing it was time to leave, she locked her door before putting the car in drive. When she looked behind herself the man had fallen onto the street, spitting awful things in the process.

"Can we get the last package on the list now please?" Valentina yelled. "And not do all this extra shit!" She slammed the steering wheel and a nail popped off. "I told you to stay on plan! I fucking told you!"

"Girl, just drive!"

The white Tesla glided smoothly through the streets of Baltimore, its sleek exterior standing out amongst the dilapidated dirty brick buildings and rundown cars parked on the curb.

As it approached Homestead, a particularly rough neighborhood in Baltimore city, Valentina, couldn't help but feel a sense of unease. Although she knew many people living in this type of environment, this was not a place for *people like her*. Besides, it was said repeatedly that she didn't know what to say out her mouth.

And so niggas wanted her dead.

When she spotted Larisa's brick red building, she pulled up to the curb but kept the engine running. Then she whipped out her keychain with the metal spiral weapon that would pierce anything, especially flesh.

Next, she opened her word app as if she were about to go to work. Maybe it was a nervous thing, but puzzles soothed her mind.

"Be quick, Larisa." Her face glowed from the screen. "I ain't spending all night out here."

She rolled her eyes.

Larisa walked confidently towards the building she inhabited, her eyes scanning the street as she went about her way. She knew this neighborhood like the back of her hand, and she wasn't afraid of the dark figures circling the white Tesla.

Correction, she wasn't afraid of *everyone*.

But one man, just one, took her heart in a bad way.

As she climbed the steps to her building, she could hear the men talking in hushed tones, their voices filled with excitement and curiosity.

"Hey, Larisa," Marcus said, his tall and lean body blended in with the graffiti on the walls like dark art. A red hat with a yellow crooked smile propped up on his head with baby dreads peeking through.

"H...hey." Larisa reached her apartment door, fumbling with her keys as she tried to unlock it.

"You good? Because I see ink on your ear."

She didn't realize that the man drew blood. "Y...yeah. I'm fine."

"And here you are, being afraid of me. When, if you look like that, shawty, there are other things to be afraid of right?"

Nah, there was a reason she feared him.

One night she came home from a club she was with Valentina in, busted drunk. She didn't even have a good time because Valentina spent hours talking about people. And how bad their hair looked or how run over their shoes were.

The next day, when she woke up in bed with a hangover so hard it temporarily blinded her to the light, she could hear voices clearly in the hallway. In agony, she rolled herself off her bed and noticed immediately that her pussy was throbbing. Bending the corner, she saw Marcus' red hat with the crooked smile sitting on the glass table.

It was the same hat that sat on his head *right now*.

When she approached him about it later, he claimed he helped her safely inside because she was lit. But she knew he helped himself to some pussy too.

And so she told her best friend Valentina.

Big mistake.

Valentina took it upon herself to do a segment on her show, while also alluding to the fact that Marcus from the neighborhood was involved. He had been labeled a rapist ever since.

And he wanted Valentina to pay.

"You not gonna stay out here and talk to me?" Marcus grinned from the hallway.

"I...I said hi. Can't that be enough?"

"You still rolling with that YouTube bitch? The one who don't know what to say out her mouth."

Silence.

"She fake as fuck...gonna get you killed." He pointed a stank weed finger her way. "And anybody you fuck with too. Watch."

Marcus pulled himself off the wall and walked in her direction. The men behind him moved closer, their footsteps echoing on the concrete. The way they carried on was one of the reasons she kept her current nigga a secret from the streets.

"Can you back the fuck up please?"

"Ain't nobody gonna touch you, girl," he chuckled.

Finally, she managed to get the door open, slipping inside and quickly locking it behind her. Looking at the door as if it were a monster which could come down at any moment, she let out a sigh of relief when it didn't.

She quickly grabbed her outfit for the night and walked back to her door with a duffle in hand and took a deep breath just as her cell rang.

It was Valentina.

"What you doing? These niggas circling my car and shit! So hurry the fuck up!"

"I'm coming now!"

CHAPTER TWO
HOOD CAVIAR

Valentina and Larisa moved packages from Valentina's car quickly into the garage of her $600,000 home in the suburbs of Baltimore county, Maryland. They had to be quick because there was a party already brewing that Valentina planned months ago, to celebrate reaching over a million subscribers across all her social media platforms.

Valentina's saying was, "The bigger the followers the bigger the finances." But it was the porch pirating that kept her life on shine.

She had a Range Rover, a Tesla, and a motorcycle she kept in storage. She owned six fur coats, ten diamond chains with pendants that sparkled with letters spelling, *Valentina* above the breasts. She also owned twenty designer pocketbooks and a bevy of designer outfits and shoes.

It was big money in thievery.

When each package was tucked inside her studio, Valentina looked out the garage and onto the street. "Did you see that car?"

"What car?"

"It was sitting in front of my house." She dipped into her pocket, popped a Percocet, and peered harder. On some wide-eyed shit she said, "It was a black Tourist Pursuit. That means police, right?"

"Nah. I ain't see it."

"Are you sure?" Her breath was heavy. "Because you did bite a man's- "

"I said nah!" Larisa wiped her mouth with the back of her hand. "Now drop it. Maybe you should leave them pills alone."

"Stop all that noise." She rolled her eyes. "Let's just go inside." Valentina attempted to go through from the garage, but Larisa blocked her. "What's wrong with you?"

"Where do you want to start?"

"Larisa, I don't have time for–."

"Marcus asked about you when I went home. And he's serious."

"Well he should've thought about that before he raped you."

"I didn't ask you to tell my story on your show though. But you didn't care because you got how many new subscribers behind that shit? Not to mention how you acted when that man grabbed me a few hours ago."

"Bitch, I told you to stay the fuck on plan! You the one wanted to get extra boxes. And when Jacob gives the money for this shit you gonna get paid. But you need to relax."

"I'm serious, Valentina. Had it not been for my mean hand game and biting his dick, we would probably be in prison right now. I mean what's wrong with you?"

"You so intent on ruining tonight. You alive."

"You acted like a punk."

Fighting words.

"Bitch, what?"

"I'm not leaving until I get two things. First a reason why you seem stuck in the weather whenever the wind blows your way. And second, my money. And don't bother telling me you'll give it to me when Jacob peels off. I want what's coming to me now."

"You know what...let me get you your little coins because you trippin'." She grabbed her Gucci, almost knocking her in the face.

"I know you crazy now. Bitch, you almost hit me!"

Stuffing her hand into her purse, she popped another nail and pulled out $400, before shoving it between Larisa's A cup breasts. "Satisfied?"

She tucked it in her pocket. "So you still not gonna tell me why you always get stuck when a little weather come through?"

"I don't know if being with my brother has you looking for answers in the stupidest of places or if living in that roach infested building got you tripping. If you don't drop it I'll–."

Larisa stepped close. "I always believed you were a bully but after tonight–."

"Don't make me–."

"What?" Larisa snapped. "Because I'm not scared of you."

"That's your problem. Because you should be."

"What about the boxes? Don't you wanna see what's inside?"

"What difference does it make? I paid you." Valentina walked around her and toward her house.

Larisa grabbed her arm, "You think everything is about you. And all you care about is yourself. One day that's gonna catch up with you when your perfect world comes crumbling down."

"Aw, girl, hush."

The chandeliers in Valentina's home were sparkling and grand, casting a warm glow over the entire space. Niggas mingled and laughed beneath the shimmering light fixtures, which were made of gleaming crystal and set in elegant, curved metal frames.

Little did they know that Valentina's extravagant lifestyle was a result of her illegal activity of porch piracy. But who cared when they could benefit on nights like this?

The sound of rap music continued to fill the air, pumping from hidden speakers built into the walls. Guests swayed and danced to the music, enjoying the party to the fullest.

Even the meal put on stunts and shows. There were a variety of delicious options including sushi, sashimi, delicate canapés, and other elegant hors d'oeuvres.

Get your own food?

Nah!

Of course she had it catered.

The staff were dressed in crisp white uniforms and were constantly refilling glasses with sparkling champagne and other beverages. They were actors, moving through the crowd with grace and efficiency, ensuring that everyone had a drink in hand and was enjoying themselves.

Wearing a black backless spaghetti strapped dress that touched the floor, the diamond chain that read *Valentina* on her neck sparkled under the soft yellow lighting throughout her home. She knew where to stand to look like she was on stage, and the light hit her right every time.

To the right of her was one of her best friend's Milo Miller. Medium ugly, his dark mocha skin and hard gaze belied a streetwise toughness that she found sexy. Everything about him was right and he used a sponge brush to keep his coils tamed while also seeing his barber on the regular.

To the left of her was Rowan Anderson who they called RoRo. The kind of man you'd find in a boy band video, his hazel brown skin with light freckles throughout added appeal to his dark personality. She wasn't as close with RoRo as she used to be, but she was hoping that with time, that would change.

All of them, RoRo, Milo, and Larisa, were fixtures in Valentina's life. Next to her brother if they acted brand new, she was fucked.

They knew her secrets.

And anybody who knew your secrets could also be called co-defendants.

When Larisa pressed her out in the past about why she wouldn't choose between RoRo and Milo, since they both cared for her and fucked her whenever she was ready, she said, *"That's the answer. Why choose one when I can have both?"* She shrugged.

"What happens when they get a girlfriend?"

"Trust me...they won't. At least, Milo anyway. RoRo been different for a year. So fuck that nigga."

And now, there they were, at her side as she celebrated a huge flex.

Having dug in her duffle, Larisa, who had freshened up in Valentina's bedroom, was now dressed in a pair of sexy fitted blue jeans and a white blouse that damn near exposed her titties.

Larisa was in front of Nevin Cash, Valentina's brother who was also Larisa's future husband. He was fine too. His neat locs were positioned throughout his scalp and he was standing behind her, with lips touching her neck as she smiled while secretly wishing he'd stop doing the most.

Including those closest to Valentina, there were twenty people present who Valentina either wanted to show off in front of or wanted to be a part of her success.

She was nothing without her fans.

Amongst them were twins, Pumpkin and Shug who these days Valentina was sure couldn't stand her guts.

At one point she fucked with them hard. Even used them to collect information to run credit card schemes. But they weren't smart and when Shug let her boyfriend use one of the cards and he got caught, he almost snitched until someone paid him a visit one night in his cell. The raised gash on his neck prevented him from saying another word.

Most knew Valentina was responsible, but no one could prove it.

The next day, Valentina dumped Pumpkin and Shug like Lori Harvey on play girl shit.

And since then, she felt they were...well raggedy.

They were standing next to the food table when Valentina walked up to them, observing their minor outfits. She was high as fuck and judgmental per usual, so this was ungood for all involved.

Pumpkin had on a pumpkin-colored jumper, which Valentina found hilarious. While Shug wore a black bodycon dress with scratched up tennis.

"Didn't y'all get the memo?" Valentina asked, wiping her hair out of her face with the hand missing a nail.

"What you talking about now?" Pumpkin asked.

"I said fly. But y'all look the fuck tired. That's what I'm talking about."

Pumpkin sighed. "We might not have the money you claim to have, but we do alright."

"Exactly, and we good with that too." Shug added.

"First off your breath smells like pussy," she pointed in Shug's face.

She frowned. "And you know how pussy smells because..."

"And you look like you picked that fit off the dust rack." She focused on Pumpkin, ignoring Shug. "Now I realize times have been hard, but how far y'all gonna fall?" She waddled away.

When she turned around, she saw Arlisa, who had been begging her for money for months.

Valentina wasn't even sure she gave her an invite, she got on her nerves so much. At the same time without her being there, her party would be weak because most people didn't fuck with Valentina.

"Valentina, did you get my text?" Arlisa walked up to her so close, her lips were next to her titties. "I really need that money to pay my rent."

She sighed. "Damn! Can you stop begging? Please."

"But I'ma get put out if–."

Valentina threw her hands up and performed loudly so everyone could hear. "Ain't you fucking somebody?"

Arlisa, embarrassed, saw the eyes upon her and said, "Never mind."

Valentina yanked her back and her face bumped into her breasts. "Nah...I'm asking for serious."

"Yeah, I got somebody."

"So why the fuck you asking other females for cash? Girl, you better step that pussy up. I'm not your sponsor."

Everybody at the party had secondhand embarrassment.

And after reading a few more folks like obituaries, Valentina switched away, raising a crystal glass in the air.

Two people got scared and walked out.

"Well, I know y'all could've been anywhere else but I appreciate you being with me tonight." She grinned. "Reaching a million subscribers ain't easy. I know a few of y'all tried." She looked directly at Shug and Pumpkin who had zero luck getting their synthetic wig business up off the ground. "Anywho, I hope to be an inspiration to all of you. And let me also be proof that if you try hard enough–."

"Girl, where is the toast?" Shug shrugged multiple times in quick succession. "'Cause you sound extra as fuck right now."

Valentina frowned.

"I mean for real. You been non-stop and–."

"I'm sorry but didn't you get what the event was about before you came?" Larisa asked.

"Meaning?"

"Meaning this is a celebration. If you east Baltimore bitches ain't feeling it, why even show up?"

"Because she's fake as fuck and I love a show!" Pumpkin responded.

"You showed up because she's fake?" Nevin asked. "Fuck kind of reason is that honey? I'm confused."

Shug and Pumpkin laughed. "There little brother goes." Shug said. "Always getting her back even though she don't give a fuck about you."

"Y'all really showing your true selves tonight," Valentina said, playing the victim. "I thought y'all could see my life and know it's possible, since we came up together and all."

They glared.

"But now I realize y'all just haters all the way around."

"What it really is, is this…you wanna keep your enemies close," Pumpkin said. "And we all know why. Don't we?"

Milo, Nevin and RoRo stared angrily.

"You know what," Valentina waved the air. "Get these whores out my house. They stinkin' up the place." Feeling annoyed, she popped a pill she was gonna take later.

Nevin and RoRo moved to escort them out.

"Don't put your fucking hand on me!" Shug said, causing them both to pause momentarily. "All I'm saying is everything about you is unoriginal." Shug said. "You don't own your house, you rent it."

"She don't even own her car," Pumpkin giggled. "She renting that too."

"Now I know you lying," Valentina boasted. "All my wheels is paid and clear."

"Yeah, well, I wonder how you came by that money."

Suddenly the heel of a shoe planted into Pumpkin's cheek so hard it nicked her skin and caused her to bleed.

It was Valentina's.

"I know you didn't just hit me with a shoe!" She moved to run in Valentina's direction.

Before shit got out of hand, Nevin and RoRo picked both up and ushered them toward the door.

"You gonna pay for this shit, bitch!" Pumpkin said kicking and screaming on her way to the curb. "Trust!"

"Fuck you and your subscribers," Shug added. "And them gnarled ass fingers of yours!" She yelled as RoRo continued to haul her out. "You can't even afford a full set!"

When their voices were gone, and Nevin and RoRo returned to her side, she took a deep breath. Raising her head high she said, "Like I was saying...thank you for celebrating my shit. Now eat, get drunk and go off! I got pills too! Who poppin'?"

Everyone who remained cheered.

The music played in the background when Valentina walked to her covered patio with a glass of wine in one hand and her word game app in the other. Her brother, Nevin, sat outside smoking a J while pillowy clouds of smoke flirted with the night sky.

When he saw her, he said, "Hey, Flapper."

She tucked the phone in her pocket. "I hate that stupid word. What does it mean again?"

"You ever seen something flap in the wind? A piece of paper hanging off a stack, thread on clothing or something like that?" He winked. "Well that's what it means. A loose end. Something that just ain't right. Just like you."

"And how does it apply again?"

"You all over the place, Valentina. And life is unraveling around you."

The wind was louder than she preferred as she looked at the tree branches swaying left and right in her yard.

He noticed. "It's not that bad, Tina. Besides, I won't let shit happen to you." He inhaled. "Have I ever?"

"I hear you little, brother." She paused. "But I'm the one who protected you all *your* life. I got you that apartment. I got you that car. Most of your gear I picked and bought. So I got you."

He shook his head. "You so pressed to get your credit that you can't even hear me."

She sighed. "I will say I miss you. But lately all your time been spent with Larisa."

"Not all of it," he sighed.

She took a deep breath and sat as far away from the outer edge of her deck as possible. Which meant she was as close to him as she could be in the moment. Slowly she rested her head on his shoulder.

"Why you out here anyway?" She asked.

"You mean outside of the fact that you got my fiancé so drunk she getting on my nerves?" She could smell the skunky odor of weed on his breath mixed with the sweet stank of liquor.

Looking behind her, into the house she saw Milo raising something in the air and Larisa and RoRo taking shots.

She put her head back. "I'll admit to the first two shots but after the sixth she lost me." She breathed in and then out. "I'm not in the mood to drink anyway."

"But you like your pills though."

She glared. "Boy, I'm grown."

"Until they make you paranoid and borderline disrespectful."

The howling wind added its input and Valentina's legs tensed up until Nevin placed his warm hand on her knee, relaxing her immediately.

"Valentina, you gotta stop gaslighting people though. You remind me of one of them niggas who ain't never had nothing and want everybody to know it."

"So you want me to turn my light out?"

"I'm not saying that. But this need to throw in nigga's faces what you do and what you got is off. And you don't have to be that way."

"It's my party, Nevin. And I–."

"Need to celebrate. That's all you gotta do. And leave the other shit alone. You get what I'm saying?" He touched her face. "People out here dealing with real shit." He looked down. "I'm dealing with real shit. And it ain't always about the materialistic. Don't grow enemies in your own backyard."

Her gut was hot with embarrassment. "Says the man who don't got shit."

"That's how you see me?"

Her diamond chain glistened in the light. "All I'm saying is I finally have the lifestyle I want, and I'm living in it hard." She looked at him. "And I ain't letting nobody take that away. Definitely not no broke ass niggas."

He shook his head. "You know what, forget I said anything."

"So I guess you want me to apologize to Pumpkin and Shug for throwing they asses out too huh?"

"Like I said, forget I ever said anything. You know everything already, remember?"

CHAPTER THREE

The guests had all gone and only Valentina and Milo remained.

As the snow continued to fall outside, Valentina sat by the fireplace, wrapped in a warm red blanket next to him. Her manicured toes, warm and cozy. She listened to the gentle rustling of the snow against the windows and watched as the flakes fluttered down, illuminated by the soft glow of street and porch lights. The world outside appeared to be a peaceful and serene winter wonderland.

And now she wanted something else.

The dick.

"Want me to help get this trash out?"

"You know I do."

Both got up and walked the trash that accumulated from the party into the garage. When it was clear enough to not annoy her, they stopped.

"The cleaning crew is coming tomorrow." She shrugged. "Let them get the rest."

"You sure? Because I don't mind."

"Yeah, Milo." She moved closer, the smell of vodka on his breath got her pussy wet because a drunk nigga meant good sex in her book. "I'm sure. I got another job for you."

"Welp, I guess I'm out," he brushed his hands together and tucked them in his back pockets.

"But I said I got another job."

"What's up with you?" Then he peered down at her with those bedroom eyes.

"I want you to tell me what you want me to know."

He frowned. "Get out of here with all that shit." He shook his head. "Ain't nobody–."

"You been halfway avoiding me all night, my nigga. I know you like I know my own body. Now spit it the fuck out before I get mad."

"Okay...I'm dating someone."

Her stomach swirled and she felt sick. She always thought he would be her thing to use sexually as she saw fit forever. But now he was changing the game.

"What you mean you *dating*? You sound like a clown."

"Well I am. And why you say it like that?"

"Because you can't handle a girl right now."

He backed up into the wall behind him, arms crossed over his body. "I'm doing just fine."

"I'm serious, Milo." She stepped closer, her voice low but intense. "The last thing you need is a girlfriend when you got me."

He looked away and shook his head. "I knew you would be this way."

"You mean telling you the truth about yourself?"

Silence.

"I mean do you love this girl or something?" She asked.

"I asked her to marry me. So that makes it a yes."

"Marry...marry...where did this come from?" She looked down and back at him. Confused. "It doesn't...it doesn't make any sense! I haven't even met her yet."

"It's happening."

Suddenly she grinned as everything became clear in her mind to hear her tell it. Pointing at him with the nail less finger she said, "Be honest...you doing this because I never wanted a relationship. And I–."

"It's not about you. It just happened. And you can't expect me to stop living while you figure shit out."

"So first RoRo starts acting different for the past year and now you think you gonna be bouncing too? Nah! It ain't happening."

"Stop acting like a nigga."

"Boy, shut the fuck up and get over here." She kissed him and used her weight to press him closer against the wall. She may have been shorter, but you would never have known. "You don't wanna marry her. What you want is this good pussy."

Although their lips connected, he pushed her back with flat palms to the chest. "Stop, girl."

She slapped his hands away. "Nigga, don't hit my hand." She moved closer and kissed him harder.

"Why you doing this all of a sudden, girl?" He moaned. "Ain't nobody playing with— "

"Touch me, Milo." She begged. "We can't do that? I mean, it ain't like you married yet."

"No, we can't be this way no more. I'm—"

He could try and fight her all he wanted.

Dropping down to her knees she quickly unzipped his pants. Before he could refute his penis was in the plushy walls of her mouth. Both warm hands worked the shaft as she made it extra hard, wet, and juicy.

Trapped, his head pinned against the wall as he looked upward. It wasn't supposed to go down like this. "Valentina, what are you...why are you doing this shit to me?"

"I just want to make you feel good," she moaned. "Before your wedding day."

To prevent himself from cumming in her mouth, he picked her up and led her to the bedroom. Pushing the door open with the weight of their bodies, he walked toward the California king sized bed with the cream pillowed headboard. And placed her down perfectly in the middle.

Once she made contact, her body went loose against the sheets. Due to where she was centered, she looked like a painting, arms in the air, legs high so he could see the pink center.

Valentina was fine, that was for sure.

She was evil too.

Wanting to ease in, he released his pants and allowed them to fall to the floor. The buckle on his belt clanked on the way down. No problem. Next, he removed her thong and lowered his body, eased on top of her, causing her to sink deeper.

"You wrong as fuck for this..." He whispered.

She giggled. "I hear you, but I feel you too." She wrapped her legs around him like handcuffs.

"This not stopping...this not..." she felt so good he couldn't finish his sentence, and she liked it that way.

In and out he moved as she clawed at his back. The more he pushed the wetter she became. They were magic together in bed. Then again, she knew that which was why she wanted him to stay. To convince him that maybe...just maybe things could be better without his new bride.

No, she didn't want commitment.

She just wanted him to stay in his place.

And that's exactly where he remained. Tucked inside her body, until the sun rose.

Valentina's face was pressed inside of her plush pillow when the sound of her phone going off woke her up. Believing Milo was still in bed, she was preparing to nudge him to hand her the device when her wrist fell heavy onto the cold sheets.

The rest of her nails were scattered around everywhere. Only 2 remained.

Raising her head slowly, which rocked due to a hangover, she saw he was gone. "Wow...he didn't even leave no money on the table." She said sarcastically.

RING...RING...

Taking the little strength she could muster, she crawled toward her cell phone which was on the side of the bed where she left him. It fell to the floor, and she had to hang halfway off to pick it up. The upside-down motion of her head made her headache more intense as blood rushed to the top. "He...hello."

"Hey."

Her face fell onto the pillow. It was him. "What you want, Milo?"

"Did you lock the door?"

"Nah...but since I'm not dead I guess that means nobody killed me." Her voice was muffled due to her head being buried in the pillow.

"Why you playing–."

"If you gave a fuck you would've used your key and locked my door. So do me a favor and drop dead."

Crawling out of bed, she went to see about her front door. But once she was out of her room, a wave of nausea hit her, and her stomach began to churn. The thought of throwing up on her expensive flooring made her move quickly towards the guest bathroom which was closest. She barely made it in time.

Once there she swung the door open, almost knocking it off the hinges. Flopping on the toilet ass first, she was able to look around while being reminded that she had a party the night before.

And they left it a mess too.

There were paper towels balled up in corners throughout and half empty cups with liquor sat on the sink and behind her along the paneling.

And was that vomit by the sink?

"These niggas gross as fuck!" She said out loud. "I can't believe they–."

Her sentence stuck in her throat when she felt her stomach churning again. In her haste to get to the bathroom she forgot she had to throw up and not piss. Holding her belly, she leaped up and got on her knees before emptying the contents in her gut which wasn't much.

Her knees stabbed into the cold floor.

That's when she saw it.

A cell phone.

Wiping her mouth with the back of her hand, she flushed and picked up the old smartphone. It wasn't an iPhone. It wasn't even a Samsung. As a matter of fact, she hadn't seen anything like it before. The material felt cheap, but no doubt good enough to make or receive calls otherwise why would it be there?

And there was a two-row keyboard below the screen.

Flushing the toilet again, with her face too close to the bowl, she felt water sprays on her chin and screamed in disgust. "Yuck!"

Wiping her face, she grabbed the phone and sat up against the wall, naked from the waist down, it was quite a scene. Shoving balled up paper towels out of the way she said, "Who would leave their cell phone?"

My phone stays with me always.

Wait...where my phone at again?

Focus, Valentina.

She was curious, but also a little wary. She didn't want to pry into someone else's business, but she couldn't shake the feeling that it was her God given right to be nosey. After all, this was her house.

And all the items inside belonged to her.

Right?

And then something hit her. If they wanted the phone so badly, they should have taken it with them. After tapping the button to awaken it, she realized it was locked.

"Of course it is."

She tried a few guesses at the passcode but had no luck.

Frustrated, and still feeling ill, she sat the phone down and was about to leave the bathroom and send a group message to everyone who showed up last night to find its owner, when she decided to keep her password skills simple.

"This shit is obviously a throw away phone, could it have a throw away passcode too?" She said out loud.

Valentina's heart raced as she realized that the phone might be some sort of secret communication. They could even be talking about her. At the very least she could call them on their shit and end all terrible friendships immediately.

And then Pumpkin and Shug entered her mind.

They were the only ones who got thrown out expeditiously. Since it was so quick, maybe one of them left it behind.

She decided to try a few basic codes. After all, she loved word puzzles, so she thought long and hard and entered a few.

Epic fail!

Finally, she looked at the keypad and looked for the letters that were a bit worn down. And then, an idea came into her mind so easily she was about to brush it off. Could the code be the word *lock*?

She wasn't sure. But she would give it a try.

5...6...2...5.

Nothing.

"Fuck!"

She took a deep breath.

"Maybe...locked?

562533.

It opened.

She dropped the phone, causing its first fracture on the screen. With her hands pressed against her face she was shocked she got inside.

Picking it up again, she quickly went to the text messages. It took five minutes to scroll to the beginning which was about eight months ago. She was flicking her thumb upward so fast she wasn't comprehending anything on the screen.

And then she reached the message that was sent the day before her party.

56

I'm gonna fuck up her life. Trust.

The words didn't make much sense. Not only that, but the names of the messengers were in code too.

Whose life was the person gonna fuck up?

It had to be her!

Her blood ran cold.

She had to tell someone.

She had to tell Larisa.

Valentina sat on her couch, scrolling through the abandoned phone. And although she called Larisa over for support, she tried several things at that point to find out who it belonged to. She even texted herself and received a message so she could track the number of the phone and the people texting.

Nothing.

They were both vanity numbers.

She did her detective work no doubt and was still short.

As she continued to lose her mind, the cleaners pushed vacuums and wiped down counters in the background. "How long they gonna be here? Because I need to know what's up."

"They not leaving until it's clean." She glared her way. "I need them to get that vomit up."

"I already told you I'm sorry," She said. "You shouldn't have given me all them shots. Now you gonna tell me what's up or not?"

Her words jolted her to the present. "You won't believe what I found last night," Valentina grabbed the bottle of wine and poured a large glass before popping a pill.

Tiny red splatters dotted the table.

One of the cleaners, an African woman, with eyes like a fly, came darting across to wipe it off immediately. The girls both gave her suspicious looks.

"She a little too good," Valentina said.

"Tell me about it." Larisa sat down next to Valentina, a curious look on her face. "Now why is the cell news?" She whispered. "And why you don't have but two fingernails left?"

"Fuck all that!" Valentina handed her the phone and pointed to the text messages with her nubs. "This conversation appears to be from two people, right? But it's like the person went out the way to hide who they texting."

"I'm listening..."

"And when I went through some of the earlier messages, at first I thought they made sense. But they don't. Most words are scrambled and don't mean anything. Most of the stuff is in code." She paused. "Except that one." She pointed to the text. "I think that one is about me. And if that one is about me, all of them are about me."

Larisa read the message.

I'm gonna fuck up her life. Trust.

She looked at her. "Hold up, you *really* think they talking about you?"

"Are you here or dead? Because I said yes!"

Larisa's eyes widened as she continued to look through the device. There were no apps and no pictures to identify the owner. Just texts. There weren't even missed calls.

"Hold up, how is it fully charged?"

"It has the same charging port as my tablet." Valentina said before snapping. "Now focus!" Another nail popped off, leaving one which she snatched off too.

"Oooh girl, you really gonna have to leave Ms. Anne alone and get a new technician." She shook her head and stared back at the phone. "Okay...and what about the numbers they texting to and from?" Larisa asked. "No information there?"

"Vanity numbers. Fakes."

"I hear you, but how do you know somebody would go through so much to get at you? Why not just send you messages directly?"

"Because that ain't how psychological games work! Plus if I get too scared, I could always go to the police and have my phone traced. But this way I don't have no legal rights to see what's up."

Larisa shook her head. "I don't know, Valley."

"I mean think about the people who be jealous, and then tell me this shit ain't about me."

"Mad at you? Maybe. Jealous? Stretching." Larisa took a deep breath. "What you gonna do?"

Valentina sighed and took a deep sip of her wine. "First I gotta find out who and why."

"True."

"Unless…"

Larisa frowned. "Unless what?"

"Unless they did it, like I said to fuck with my mind. Like on the show."

Larisa put a comforting arm around Valentina. "I need you to pace yourself, Valentina. In case you take it too far like you have in the past."

"I think somebody may be trying to *An Ugly Girl's Diary Me*!" She paused. "It makes perfect sense! Everybody knows I love that show!"

Larisa rolled her eyes and removed her arm. "Not that fucking podcast again."

"All the details add up!" She positioned her body to look into her eyes. "It was left in my bathroom with a code that was easy to unlock. Like I said, I think they wanted me to find it before--."

"Before what?"

"Before they ruin my life. Just like Courtney did with Tye Gates when she had a fake diary deposited in his car. Somebody is going to the police."

"Hold up, didn't you tell me the diary was actually about the person who found it? Like, didn't he fuck up the girl's life first which is why she got revenge?"

"Yes! And if they think I'm going out like Tye they got me fucked up!"

"But he deserved the shit he had happen to him. Right? Took her money. Had her son put in foster care. She was broken down behind that nigga. Are you saying you just as foul?"

"No! I'm saying niggas is jealous. There's a difference. And I peeped how you sound like a fan."

Larisa shook her head. "I can see this is about to go left because you doing the most. You want me to stay with you tonight?"

"What about my brother? You know he don't like you out all night."

"We don't live together and he gonna be 'aight. But I gotta talk you out of this shit before you go too far."

Valentina nodded. "Yeah...stay. I don't think I could be alone right now."

"So what you wanna do?"

"Try and decipher the messages. Starting with this   word.   I   mean,   what   is   a, *iff...luy...micy...wonka?*"

"Like the wonka factory?"

"Nah, Larisa. This ain't a fucking game."

"Welp, pour out the wine," Larisa said, sitting back. "It's gonna be a long night. Who you think are the main culprits?"

Valentina popped another pill. "Shug, Pumpkin, Milo and RoRo." She fell back. "RoRo been acting different, so I'ma start with him first."

"And Marcus?" Larisa added.

"Nah, because how could he get in my house?"

"The same way he got in mine." They looked at the wine. "When you was drunk."

CHAPTER FOUR
MOVIES, POPCORN & LIES

Valentina stood in line at the movie theater, huddled under her red and green Gucci umbrella as the rain poured down around her and RoRo. She could do without the weather but there was no wind, so she was cool.

For now.

The entire night, she felt RoRo was trying to be on his best, but she was suspicious of everybody ever since she found that phone in her bathroom.

She had twenty people there and not one of them asked for their shit.

As the thunder slapped the sky, she glanced over at RoRo, who was standing a few feet away from her, chatting on his cell.

As the line inched forward to enter the theater, Valentina's nerves began to get the better of her. She fiddled with the handle of her umbrella, trying to work up the courage to confront him about the cell phone or his possible involvement with the police.

But before she could, he ended the call, turned, and said, "You good? Because you been looking at me like you wanna say something all night. Now what's up?"

She swallowed. "Can I trust you?"

They moved closer toward the entrance. "You really gotta ask?"

Yeah, nigga. She thought.

"Can I trust you, RoRo?" She repeated.

He bent down and kissed her cheek. "Stop playing with me."

Why you not answering nigga?

Valentina forced a smile and nodded, still feeling uneasy. The rest of the line went by in a blur, and before she knew it, they were at the front, buying tickets and finding their seats in the crowded theater for the blockbuster movie, *The Gods Of Everything Else.*

As the previews began to play, Valentina couldn't focus on anything but him. She kept sneaking glances out of the corner of her eye, trying to gauge his mood.

Nothing.

But as the movie started, RoRo reached over and took her hand, giving it a reassuring squeeze. "Things gonna be better. Between us."

Valentina relaxed a little, feeling a sense of relief wash over her. Maybe he didn't leave the phone after all.

"RoRo..."

He grabbed some buttery popcorn and tossed it in his mouth. "Yeah?"

"Did you leave anything at my house?"

He kissed her cheek, but his gaze was on the movie which had started with young Banks Wales and his mother in a car outside of a liquor store. "Listen, no matter what we do or what happens, I will always care about you. Don't worry."

She was kind of relieved...

And then she replayed what he said...*"no matter what we do or what happens, I will always care about you. Don't worry."*

What the fuck?

CHAPTER FIVE
FLY OVER HEAD

After not being able to feel RoRo out she decided to get with Milo instead. Luckily for her he called and invited her out for dinner, picnic style in his car.

He had a fetish for watching planes take off at a hangar because deep down Milo, himself, wanted to learn to fly but he never built up the courage.

A player since the day he was born, Milo brought a basket with finger sandwiches, fresh fruit, and wine. Since he had a sky roof in his old car, they could plane watch and whenever they did, Milo was in heaven.

They did this kind of thing since they were kids.

He and Valentina sat in the back seat, her long hair cascading over her shoulders like a waterfall. The cool air rushing inside but getting knocked away due to the blowing heat. A faint smile played on his lips as he watched each plane take off.

As they soared, Milo reached over and took Valentina's hand, giving it a gentle squeeze. "I'm glad we're doing this," he said, his voice laced with emotion and guilt. And she picked up on all that shit. "It's been too long since we've had a chance to just sit and watch the world go by. Without turning everything to the bedroom."

I like the bedroom. She thought.

As the last plane vanished into the distance, Milo turned to Valentina, his eyes sparkling. "Just 'cause I'm getting married doesn't mean we can't still be friends."

"Let's not talk about her, Milo," Valentina replied, leaning in to kiss him softly on the lips. "Because I'm gonna always be first and I know you care about me."

"More than anything. And I'm sorry about...you know, leaving your crib without locking the door. I just had to...you know, get back to her before she started asking questions and shit."

It was time to go deeper. "Did you leave anything else when you left?"

"Anything else like what?"

"Answer."

"First off, I took everything I needed." He winked and looked through the sunroof.

She needed to get even deeper.

"Milo," she said, her voice barely above a whisper. "There's something I need to talk to you about."

Milo focused on the seriousness in Valentina's eyes. "I'm listening, shawty."

"I don't know if I can trust you. I know you've always been there for me, but lately I've been feeling like you're hiding something. And this is not about your fiancé'."

"I get it now," he said, taking her hand in his. "It's about your party, right?"

So your bitch ass did leave that phone!

Valentina's eyes narrowed as she looked at Milo, her heart pounding in her chest. After all, she hadn't expected to solve the case so quickly. "Is it?" She whispered. "You tell me."

"First let me say since the moment I met you–."

"Just get to it!"

He was embarrassed. "I'm the reason Pumpkin and Shug went off on you at your party."

She frowned. "What you talking about?"

"I was having a conversation on the phone about your business, and they overheard me. With my friend and–"

"So basically you were talking behind my back? About shit I do in the street?" She leaned closer. "Or about something else?"

Silence.

"Wow." She shook her head. "So you a jealous ass nigga. That's what you saying?!"

"Why you going left? After I bought you wine and shit?"

"I can purchase my own wine and cheese cubes. I'm asking you a firm question, bruh."

"I could never be jealous of you."

"Then what was the reason for talking about me in the first place?"

Silence.

"Milo, open your fucking mouth! You ain't have no problem doing it earlier."

"I'm not jealous...I got drunk and I just feel like you brag too much."

"Brag for what?"

"When you came in the other night for your party, the first thing you did was tell people how much you spent for the caterers. Then you talked about the money you spent on your clothes. And how you did Arlisa was tragic."

"So you're at my party, talking about me to your dumb ass fiancé' and I'm supposed to give a fuck 'bout Arlisa?"

"I said a bunch of shit and that's all you heard."

"You know what...I'm glad I know how you really feel."

"All I'ma say is this, I think you need to change your ways. Or somebody may bring up the past."

The bass thumped through the walls of the crowded establishment, rattling the glasses on the shelves. The air was thick as Valentina sat pretty at the bar. People were loud as fuck, but not noisy enough to prevent her from making a call.

"Larisa, the nigga ain't let on about shit."

"I told you. Let me go on record by saying it could still just be a cell phone."

"Nah...I think I'm on to something. But I'ma follow up with him later."

"Please let it go...I got some more addresses for–."

"I can't do no jobs until I know I'm not about to get locked up."

"I hear you. I guess I'll save my money and make do." She sighed. "So where you at with the plan now?"

"About to go see a dog."

Valentina entered the Japanese steakhouse like a gust of fresh air, her designer heels clicking against the marble floor.

Heads turned as she passed, admiring the way the light caught the delicate fabric of her dress, hugging her curves in all the right places. Her hair fell in soft waves over her shoulders and her lips were painted a luscious shade of red. In one hand, she held a designer purse from Hermes, its iconic orange hue adding a pop of color to her already stunning outfit.

She looked this fucking good, just to cuss a nigga out.

Impatient as a two-month-old baby, she searched for Pumpkin, and spotted her sitting regally at a corner table, head held high, and hands folded.

Valentina quickly approached and plopped down in front of her, causing soy sauce to splatter on her bag. "Do you have anything to say to me, bitch?" Valentina said through clenched teeth.

Pumpkin dabbed at the mess she made with a napkin before looking her square on. "I see you got your nails did."

"Waiting!"

"As far as something to say, I think that's the other way around," she said, her voice steady. "I mean look at my face! You hit me with a shoe."

The smell of sizzling steak and the sound of clanking knives and forks filled the air as the chefs cooked at the grill in the center of the room. If either of the ladies got too crazy, a knife may come flying their way.

Valentina leaned closer; her eyes narrowed. "How you carried on at my party was disrespectful. So you had it coming."

"Hold up, you act like it was your birthday or something. Don't nobody give a fuck about no subscribers."

"What I want to know is this, are you working with the police or not?"

"Police?" Pumpkin glared. "I don't know what you talking about, but if your ass gets locked up you deserve it. Because we both know where the real money coming from don't we?" She giggled.

Valentina shook her head, her eyes filled with anger. "You foul, Pumpkin. And I thought we were friends."

Pumpkin leaned back in her chair, her expression unyielding. "If you not gonna apologize to me for throwing a shoe, get the fuck out my face."

"Why would I apologize? I gave you life...literally. It's 'cause of me you in that house. It's 'cause of me your sister got that raggedy ass Benz. If anything, y'all should be licking my dirty panties clean."

"All that money and you can't wash your clothes?"

"You know what, that's why Arlisa fucking your man," Valentina added.

"Bitch, you sound crazy!" She paused. "And I know you better get out my face now before I hurt you."

Valentina stood up slowly, her chair scraping against the floor, her eyes filled with disappointment. "I'll be in contact."

"Is that a threat? If it is, you crazy because you forgot who I am."

Valentina grabbed her spotted bag, and stormed away from the table, leaving Pumpkin sitting alone.

TWO DAYS LATER

Valentina hastily hurried through the mall parking lot; her arms clenched tightly around shopping bags. Bad moods always sent her to the cash register. Lost in thought, she failed to notice the ominous figures lurking in the shadows until it was too late.

With a sudden pounce, Shug and Pumpkin appeared from behind a parked car, their faces contorted with malice. "You think you better than us?!" Shug yelled.

Panic set in as Valentina realized the gravity of the situation.

She tried to retreat, but Pumpkin seized her by her hair, yanking her forward. "You got a big mouth, bitch," Pumpkin growled, tightening her grip. "Where is the energy you had at the party?"

Before she could even scream for help, they launched their vicious jealousy fueled attack.

Valentina's pleas were muffled by the sounds of cars rushing by and the chatter of indifferent people who could care less about her little crook life.

At the end of the day, not a single person came to her rescue.

With cruel enjoyment, Shug and Pumpkin relentlessly pummeled Valentina to the ice-cold ground, their fists and feet raining down on her.

After what seemed like forever, she felt a searing pain in her eye, and a sharp sting in her lip as it split open.

Battered and bloodied, she crumpled to the pavement, helpless and alone.

"Just like I thought. All mouth no game." Shug said.

As they walked away, laughing in triumph, Valentina was left to suffer.

She lay there for what felt like an eternity, her mind numb with shock and her body writhing in pain.

Eventually, someone discovered her and called for help, but the damage was done, and done well.

Fueled by a burning rage, Valentina swore to make Shug and Pumpkin pay for what they had done.

And that was on everything.

CHAPTER SIX
PRETTY BRUISED

This phone was ruining her fucking life...

Valentina's gold bangle earrings sparkled as she sat at a small table in an ice cream parlor with her eyes fixed on the raindrops running down the window.

The fog outside blurred the view of her car sitting on the street, giving the impression of a never-ending gray void. It didn't help that her eye was blackened, and her lip was busted courtesy of Pumpkin and Shug.

Since she set out for answers, all she seemed to get was whooped.

Milo stopped answering his phone and RoRo once again disappeared. This was making her more noid.

The bruises looked so out of place against the Cuban link necklace above her cleavage, that people gawked as they passed thinking it was a poor makeup job.

"You got a problem?" She yelled at a woman and her child, as she busied herself in her black Hermes' purse. "Because I can fix that shit for both of you if need be." She stuffed an earbud inside her canal.

"I hope you had the same energy for whoever kicked your ass."

She didn't.

"Bitch, get out my face." She stuffed the next one and grabbed her phone to hit her show.

The woman shook her head and walked out.

As she focused on the podcast trying to get ideas for her next move, she absently stirred her melting ice cream with a spoon while the show blasted through her earbuds.

The sound of the narrator's voice and the occasional bursts of laughter from the podcast blended with the soft chatter of the customers and the clinking of spoons against glass bowls relaxed her.

A little.

A slight smile played on her lips as she focused on the next guest in the latest episode of *An Ugly Girl's Diary*. Today's guest followed the story of a woman named Playana, whose boyfriend had just left her for her co-worker. And she was on the show trying to get some tips on how she could seek revenge.

Valentina could relate to her heartbreak and feelings of betrayal. The last man she loved left her while she was in the hospital due to an untreated yeast infection which spread to other organs in her body. When she came home he had packed up everything and was gone.

She was soon evicted.

As she listened, Valentina felt a sense of comfort knowing that she wasn't alone in her own struggles.

The way the host, Courtney, was able to get raw and honest storytelling out of her guests was something that Valentina appreciated and found cathartic. It was like having a friend to confide in, even though they had never met in person.

As the episode ended, Valentina felt grateful for the solace that the podcast brought her. But now it was time to get focused.

Ten minutes later, she glanced up as Jacob walked in and a look of relief crossed her face.

He was a tall and muscular man, standing at 6'4" with broad shoulders. Head shaven, and a small scar above his left eyebrow, the plain white t-shirt he sported was creased in the middle, indicating it left its family of a fresh pack recently.

He had a rough exterior, which he earned from his past as a boxer, and it made him look extra menacing and fine at the same damn time.

"Hey, J," she said, standing up to greet him.

He shoved her back down with a heavy hand on her shoulder. "You drawing fucking attention." He looked around and back at her face. "Anyway, what happened to you?" He took a seat.

"I'm okay," Valentina said, waving a hand dismissively.

"You sure?"

"Like you care."

He cleared his throat. "What you need?"

"A big ass favor. You know that package I asked for?"

He stared at her like she was dumb.

Of course he knew, it was the only reason he agreed to see her beautiful ass in the first place. Because at the end of the day, Valentina was trouble.

"Yeah...still don't get it." He whispered. "I ain't know you to ever push dope."

"I'm not. I need you to take it to Shug's house and leave it in her car."

He frowned and wiped a hand down his chin. It fell heavily in his lap. "I thought y'all were friends."

"Nah."

"You always starting shit." He sat back shaking his head. "And how the fuck am I supposed to get inside anyway?"

"The back door lock is broken. She too cheap and talk too much shit to get it fixed. That's your in."

He shook his head. "The paper. Where it at?"

She was preparing to hand him the money across the table until, "Under...not over." His teeth were clenched.

"My bad."

She reached down and did as he said. She wasn't sure if he got it until he snatched the bag so hard it almost pulled her arm out of her socket. Next, he tucked it in the front of his pants, giving himself an even bigger dick print.

"I'll take care of it." He mumbled. He rose and turned to leave, his mind racing with questions about why Valentina couldn't take it to Shug's herself.

As he bopped through the parlor, the patrons couldn't help but stare at him, some with a look of fear and others with a look of admiration. But he paid them no mind and continued out of the parlor to do her dirty work.

Something that had become custom for them. It was literally the only thing that kept them together.

After all, he was the man who had left her when she was sick in the hospital with a bad yeast infection.

And he still couldn't get her out of his life.

An hour later, she was still in the ice cream shop when the cashier walked over. She had a fluffy red ponytail and glasses with a crack on the right lens. "Ain't that much ice cream in the world."

"Bitch, what?" Valentina said as she paused using her laptop.

"Are you still eating or using our wi-fi? Because free ain't free."

"You know what..." Valentina dug in her pocket and shoved a fifty on her pudgy belly. "Now leave me the fuck alone."

"Well what you want to order?"

"Sis...go back there, put twenty scoops in a trashcan and you eat it."

The woman rolled her eyes. "Stupid bitch," she said before walking away.

Fifteen minutes later, her cell phone rang. "Done."

Jacob's voice was like music to her ears.

Now it was time to make her next move.

Shug snuggled into the soft cushions of the sofa, her head resting on Q's shoulder. The TV's blue radiance casted a warm glow over the room. Outside, a gentle snowfall blanketed the city, adding to the coziness of the moment.

Q brushed a strand of hair from Shug's forehead and placed a soft kiss on her temple. "You know, I'm grateful we got back together," he said.

Shug smiled and nestled closer. "You always talking shit when you want some pussy."

"Is it working?"

Q may have been happy she took him back after getting caught fucking his neighbor, but she had a reason.

When it was good, he helped her see the beauty in the world when all she could see was darkness. He had been her rock through some of the toughest times she faced, especially when Valentina cut her off and she couldn't pay her bills.

He was a classically trained nigga.

Knew all the right words and held a decent dick game. He knew how to spend just enough time to get her loyalty, and sneaky enough not to get caught too often fucking something else on the side.

"Did you get with Arlisa?"

"I said no. She ain't my type. And you know that." Q's hand brushed over the back of hers, eliciting a shiver from Shug. He looked down at her, a soft smile playing on his lips. "Now you gonna kiss it first?" He asked.

Shug giggled. "Just like that huh?"

Q chuckled. "You want me to beg? Because I'm being honest when I say, I ain't never met a woman who can lick the tip like you."

"Where is the compliment?"

"If you feeling insulted then you just don't see how much I can't be without you."

Shug's heart skipped a beat at his words. Hood niggas had the code to hood women and it was as simple as that.

"Q," she said, her voice filled with emotion, "I love you. If we gonna be together...you gotta do right. All the time. Not some time."

Of course he was still gonna cheat.

This was all semantics. Like a public defender speaking for his client that he was sending straight to jail.

Q pressed his lips to hers in a soft, sweet kiss. "I'm done stepping out on you, girl. Now lick that thing...it belongs to you."

Slowly she eased up and positioned herself between his legs like a piece in a puzzle. Next, she unfastened his buckle and pulled down the golden clasp to his zipper. His head fell back as he waited to feel what them lips do. Her tongue was cool at first before warming the shaft.

Cuffing his balls, she moved them up and down while bobbing like ocean waves. He widened his legs so he could push upward into her throat just right, without choking her too much.

Of course he reserved the right to get nastier later.

Q almost reached an orgasm when they were interrupted by a loud knock on the door. They both froze, fear creeping into their hearts. After all, they had pasts so one couldn't be sure.

Q grabbed his gun on the side of the couch until she stopped him.

"I don't move like that no more, baby."

"You might not, but it don't mean somebody else don't." He whispered. "Plus this one legal."

"It may be legal but I'm a felon and you don't live here." She paused. "Just let me see what's up. I'm not supposed to be around that gun. It sounds like the beat of the police." She wiped her mouth with the back of her hand while he slipped back into his jeans.

Q tucked the gun in the couch cushions in case it was the cops.

The knock grew louder and sure enough when she opened it, two officers stuffed themselves inside of her house like they owned 51% of everything.

"Hold the fuck up!" She yelled. "What's going on?"

"Shug Jones?" One of the officers asked, his eyes flicking back and forth between her and Q.

His hand also hovered over his weapon and his partner followed suit.

"Yeah...that's me." Shug said, her voice trembling, hands high in the air. "But what the fuck is this about?"

"We have a warrant to search your car."

"My car! What the fuck for?"

"We received a tip," the officer said, holding out a piece of paper. "That you out here selling drugs in your community."

She stepped back and dragged a hand down her face. She figured it was one of her neighbors doing their best to get her evicted from her rental because of the loud music and the company she kept. "But I don't do shit like that no more! I been out the game for years. I ain't trying to–."

"Well if you really are out, it won't make a difference if we search, will it?"

She thought about Q's gun being hidden in her sofa again and decided to relent. "Nah...I can let you check my Benz."

Q and Shug exchanged worried looks. "You stay right here." They pointed at Q.

He crossed his arms over his chest and planted in the living room.

Worried, she followed the officers outside, her mind racing with questions.

Who could have called the police?

And why were they fucking with her tonight when she was clean?

The moment the cops entered the car, dug under the seat and pulled out a pack her knees went weak. It was a set up and she knew it. "Hold the fuck up! That's not mine!"

"Yeah whatever." The officer said. "Cuff her ass."

Shug stumbled as the officers roughly grabbed her arms and yanked them behind her back, the cold metal of the handcuffs biting into her skin. Her bare feet scraped against the snow-covered pavement, leaving behind a trail of icy footprints.

Shug's eyes stung with tears as she tried to take in her surroundings, her mind racing with fear and confusion.

She could see the bright flashing lights of the police vehicle, reflecting off the dark windows of nearby houses. A crowd had gathered, curious onlookers craning their necks to get a glimpse of what was happening.

She was sure it was one of them bitches for certain who made the call. They had been trying to get her out for months.

The officers roughly shoved her into the back seat of the car, the door slamming shut with a loud bang. The smell of stale coffee and musty upholstery filled her nose as she slumped down on the seat, her heart racing, and her mind numb with shock.

As the car pulled away from the curb, Shug could feel the rough texture of the handcuffs rubbing against her skin. The sound of the engine roared in her ears, drowning out the shouting of the crowd outside. She closed her eyes, tears streaming down her face as she tried to make sense of what was happening.

And then it all became clear.

This was no damn neighbor!

This was Valentina Cash's work.

CHAPTER SEVEN
TOO CLOSE

Standing at the kiosk, Valentina checked Shug off the list. With her in jail the last thing she would be for her was trouble. So she decided to direct her energy back to RoRo. She would see every nigga with a name framed and behind bars before she let them lock her up instead.

And so, Valentina nervously followed RoRo in her Tesla as he stormed through the bustling city streets, her heart pounding inside her chest because she had no idea where he was going or what he was planning. But she knew that she couldn't just let him move about the world anymore with her not watching.

But when they turned into a dark and shadowy parking lot, Valentina's anxiety ticked up a few levels. She tried to provide space but if he turned his head she would be seen for sure. So when he parked further away, she positioned her car so far it was *almost* impossible to keep him in view.

Being from Bmore, and in connection with her creep game, she saw his ass good enough.

Easing out of the car, quietly, she hung back, trying to stay out of sight as RoRo approached a shady looking stranger leaning against a beat-up old car. The man was tall, handsome enough and wearing blue jeans, a white t-shirt, and a black blazer.

Although she hoped for more information on why RoRo was being elusive, after five minutes, she was starting to get bored.

And then it dawned on her, could he be police?

Things got stranger when suddenly they began to argue, their voices growing louder and more heated with each passing moment. Valentina couldn't make out what they were saying, but she could tell that whatever it was, it was important enough to get violent.

As the argument came to a climax, Valentina watched in horror as RoRo reached into his pocket and pulled out a small, shiny object.

"Hold up, is that a fucking gun?" She said to herself.

The stranger backed away and into another car. His hands rose in the air, and he spoke to RoRo in a way that made him lower the weapon.

Suddenly, the stranger lunged at RoRo, his hand flashing out and snatching the object from his grasp. RoRo yelled something that was inaudible as the man hollered back.

"Fucks this about?" She said to herself. "I don't get it."

RoRo wasn't selling drugs anymore, so why such an intense interaction?

Needing someone to help her sort things out, she fumbled for her phone and quickly dialed Larisa's number, hoping she would answer.

She did.

"Larisa, it's me," she whispered as soon as she picked up. "I'm in a parking lot and there's this man here with RoRo. And...and they out here arguing and shit."

"About what?"

"I don't know but I'm really scared because it could be police. Do you think they talking about me? Do you think...think...hold on." She reached in her glove compartment, popped a pill, and held the phone to her ear. "I'm back."

"Valentina, I told you not to press this shit. It could be something totally different. Do you see how you making a big thing out of a cell phone? Do you see this shit?"

"I'm telling you it doesn't look good. Who is this dude?"

Larisa took a deep breath. "Okay...I mean...are you okay?" Her voice was filled with concern and irritation in the same mix. "Where are you? Meet me."

"I'm on the east side." She then proceeded to describe the man in full detail, just in case something happened.

"Okay, go to James Pawn Shop. It's my uncle's."

"I'm on my way," Valentina said firmly.

"If you get there before I do, don't leave. I'll be there."

Valentina did as she was told, her heart racing as she watched RoRo and the man continue to argue while she pulled off as quietly as possible. Hopefully without being detected.

Picking up her phone she hit Jacob. "It's me."

"I know."

"Can I see you?"

"How much? And what's the job?"

She sighed. "No...I'm asking can you...can I *see* you?"

He paused. "If I agree, all you getting is that. Can you handle it?"

"I need you. So the answer is yes."

After begging him to see her, she made her way to the pawn shop. Parking her car, Valentina walked into the dimly lit business, the neon sign outside casting a flickering light on her face.

She took a deep breath, trying to shake off the feeling that the man RoRo met was police. The musty smell of old merchandise and the sound of the bell ringing as customers came and went did little to calm her nerves.

Was she taking too many pills after all?

Nah.

She was good to hear her tell it.

Slowly she moved over to the glass display cases filled with jewelry, watches, musical instruments, electronics, and more. She tried to distract herself by looking at the goods, but her mind kept going back to RoRo.

After what felt like an eternity, Larsia walked in and rushed over to where Valentina was waiting. Grabbing her by the hand she said, "Come on, let's get out of here."

"But I thought you wanted to talk."

"No...I wanted you to wait here. But you coming with me now."

Valentina's head leaned against the cool window when she received a text message on her personal cell phone from a number she didn't recognize. It read:

December 4th
TEXT: Let it go. Now.

Quickly she removed the other phone from her pocket, the one she found in her bathroom.

And the last message was still the same.

I'm gonna fuck up her life. Trust.

Oh nah...she was right.

Someone was out to get her.

Larisa had been driving for an hour and now Valentina felt like the car was closing her up after receiving a new message on her personal number. "Pull over."

"But you said to drive as far away as–."

"Pull the fuck over, bitch! At that park!" She pointed across her. "Please."

Larisa took a deep breath and did what she was told.

When the car was parked, they walked around for a little while in silence and then Valentina uttered, "I...I want to go home now."

"You haven't even talked about why this shit got you so frazzled. At least tell me something so I can understand–."

"Please stop."

Larisa sighed. "I think you getting worked up for nothing. Now I want to know what the fuck is going on?"

Valentina looked at her angrily. "I did something."

"Like what?"

"I did something to Shug. And now I'm getting a text on my personal cell."

Larisa looked as if the color had drained from her skin. "Are you serious? Are you fucking serious?! That bitch is crazy. What did you do?"

"I set her up. Had Jacob put drugs in her car. Then I called the neighborhood watch folks who couldn't stand her and they hit up the police And now–."

"YOU DID WHAT?" Larisa touched the sides of her head. "I think you losing your mind over a fucking phone! If you think somebody gonna tell police what you do, stop!"

"It's not that easy."

"Why isn't it? Tell me why you really scared of the police. Because it's not about porch pirating. I feel it in my heart."

She shuffled a little. "Well...what...what else would it be about?"

As they turned the corner onto the street where Larisa's car was parked, Valentina noticed a figure standing in the shadows, watching them intently. Her heart raced as she tried to see if it was the stranger from the parking lot.

"Don't look quick but do you see that man?" Valentina whispered to Larisa. "Over there."

Larisa's eyes narrowed as she peered at the figure. "You mean the one waiting by that car?"

"That's what you call it? Waiting?"

"What you call it?"

"I think he's the nigga from the lot and now he's following me."

"But you said the man had on a blazer and–."

"So he can't change his fucking clothes? At my party you put on four outfits. One of them was mine."

"Bitch, calm down! There are kids in that park, Valentina. Maybe–."

"Just be quiet!"

Valentina's mind raced as she debated what to do next. Should they turn back and call an Uber? Leaving Larisa to drive home alone.

"Just take me back to my car."

"Good," Larisa sighed. "Because I can't with all this extra shit!"

As they approached Larisa's ride, the figure stepped out of the shadows and into the light. It was a man, tall and muscular with a stern expression on his face. Since she was scared but wanted to know more, she felt it best to step to him.

"Who are you?" Valentina demanded, trying to sound braver than she felt. "Huh? And why the fuck you following us?"

"Girl, what are you doing?" Larisa said, tugging her coat.

The man remained silent but did continue to stare.

"Who are you?" Valentina yelled again, with her hand on the passenger's side door. "I asked you a legit question!"

The man didn't answer but walked slowly toward them.

Oh no!

Now Larisa was scared.

Valentina's heart pounded in her chest as they fumbled with the door, finally managing to get inside. The moment they were safely in, a woman and three kids walked up to the man and began signing.

They were hearing impaired.

So they couldn't hear a word Valentina said.

"You did all that shit for nothing!" Larisa yelled. "Can you let this go now? Please."

Valentina took a deep breath and shook her head slowly from left to right. Tears streamed down her cheeks. "I can't...I'm...I'm sorry. I gotta know what's up."

"If that's how you feel, hear my words. This thing you got going on, whatever it is, gonna cause a lot of people to get hurt. It already has. I hope you're ready for that shit."

They pulled down the street, not realizing that the man who was fighting with RoRo in the garage, had been parked behind them the entire time.

Valentina was right to be afraid.

She just picked the wrong perpetrator.

DECEMBER 5th

TEXT: In high school U were dumb 2. I C ain't shit changed. I left a whole phone in your house, and U still can't unlock the truth. But we know why U scared. :)

After reading the text on her personal phone, that seemed to be coming more frequently, Valentina needed a relief.

And so, she walked into the dingy motel room, her heels clicking on the stained linoleum floor just to get her clit flipped. The room was small and cramped, with peeling wallpaper and a musty smell that made her nose wrinkle in disgust.

Jacob loved incognito.

He liked grime.

She didn't mind it either when she was with him.

She pushed aside her revulsion and focused on the man sitting at the table in the center of the room.

The light glowing on his face.

"What do you want?" He asked, his voice low.

Valentina took a deep breath, trying to steady her nerves. "I miss you," she said softly. "And I ain't got nobody else right now."

Jacob raised an eyebrow. "That's not why we here."

Valentina walked over and sat down across from him. She could feel his eyes on her, and she knew that he was still as attracted to her despite his rudeness.

"I know it's hard, but when we meet in places like this, can we at least pretend? Since I'm paying you?" She said, her voice barely above a whisper.

"Pretend what?"

"That you still love me."

Jacob leaned forward; his eyes narrowed.

Valentina reached across the table and took his hand. "I'm lonely, Jacob. I been that way since you left and–."

"You know why I left."

She looked down. "I do."

Jacob pulled his hand away. "I'm not the same person I was when you were mine."

That shit hurt.

Slowly she rose.

"I don't believe you." Starting with her fur coat, she removed each piece of clothing as they fell into piles at her bare feet.

Walking over to him, she placed one leg over to the right and then left, as she straddled him while peering down into his eyes. His cool hands touched the small of her back.

"You still love me." She kissed his lips and then his neck. He smelled so good and strong. "Don't lie, J."

"What makes you believe that shit?" The rumble of his voice in her ear reached down to her glistening button.

"Because when we're like this, the hate for what I do goes away, and I see the love for me in your eyes."

With one hand on her waist, he released his thickness from his pants. Slowly he eased into her, causing her to float higher off her feet like she was on a carousel. Up and down she moved in a rhythmic flow.

Their lips met one another as he panted heavily.

Jacob was hardcore, so she loved that she could still make him make such a primitive sound. "Damn...you so wet."

"Am I the one?" She said, feeling herself on the verge of reaching an orgasm. "Am I the one?"

"When we like this, I can't even front. But it's not enough."

TWO DAYS LATER
DECEMBER 7th
TEXT: How it feel to know your time is up? And to think, you so far from the truth you wrong.

Valentina's hand shook as she filled the kettle with water and placed it on the stove. The darkness outside and the eerie silence only added to her anxiety, and she needed relief.

She sat down at the kitchen table, trying to steady her breathing. It was kinda working or whatever. Just as she was starting to feel a little better, she received another text message.

U wanna fuck with me? Now I'ma fuck with U.

Her eyes widened and then, her phone rang.

She hesitated for a moment before answering. It was a collect call from Shug, who was in prison on account of some shit she did.

Valentina, curious, decided to accept it.

"Valentina," her voice came through the receiver, "You gonna pay. You hear me...I mean that shit, bitch."

Valentina swallowed. "Shug? I don't know what you're talking about," she stammered. "I haven't seen you in months." She lied. "Maybe you should get your mental health checked because–"

"Ain't nobody crazy but you, bitch! I should've told the police how–."

CLICK.

Valentina hung up. There was no way she was going to allow her to get her hemmed up on a recorded line.

She decided to call Milo.

He didn't answer.

Next, she called RoRo. He answered but said, "Now ain't the right time."

"Why not?"

"Because I'm busy."

She ended the call. "Sure you are," she said to herself.

With a scattered mind, she eased up from the table and walked over to the window, peeking through the blinds. The street was empty and dark, but she saw something.

A red hat.

Sitting on her front lawn.

The kettle whistled, and she accidentally knocked it over, burning her arm in the process.

"FUCK!"

CHAPTER EIGHT
UP TO TROUBLE

DECEMBER 8th

TEXT: Your shit has caught up with U, and there's no escaping the truth. I can't wait 2 celebrate your demise when it's all said and done.

Last night was not her night...

Her face was healing but still fucked up, arm was now burned and wrapped in a bandage, and she was losing her mind. But she couldn't focus on any of it. Besides, there was more work to do.

Valentina stood on the sidewalk, watching as RoRo walked out the bank and turned down the street. She quickly crossed the road, keeping a safe distance as she followed him. She wondered if he was going to meet the stranger from the parking lot, but for real she couldn't be sure.

One thing was certain that he was slipping. RoRo was so focused on whatever was on his mind that he didn't even look back to see her there. What if she wanted to kill his ass?

As he walked, Valentina kept her eyes on him, trying to stay hidden behind a group of people that were also walking down the street. They were loud but their voices faded into the background of the city.

Eventually, they reached the light rail station and RoRo descended the stairs. Making sure not to lose him, Valentina followed closely, while keeping a safe distance.

Next, he bought a go pass to get on the train, still unaware of his surroundings. Valentina quickly did the same and made her way to the platform just in time to see his train pulling up.

The moment he got on, she got on too, many doors down.

He took a seat, rows ahead, while she tucked herself in the back and pulled out her cell to give play by play. "Hey, it's me," she said to Larisa. "I'm on the train right now, following RoRo. He just went into some bank and now he's on his way somewhere else. I don't know where but something's up."

Silence.

"Anyway, he probably getting off downtown. He's–"

"You getting on my fucking nerves! I mean, leave that man alone, please! This is ridiculous."

"Girl, why you yelling?"

Larisa continued to tell her all the reasons why she shouldn't follow RoRo. And although Valentina listened, it was clear she made her mind up a long time ago and had no intention of changing.

"Just so you know, Shug is out for you. She even told somebody she wanted to talk to me about something. And we ain't never been cool."

She sat up straight. "Wait...what? She called you?"

"Yeah...my friend said she sounded angry."

"You shouldn't listen to her. I wouldn't even answer the phone. She out here fucking with my mind even though she locked up. But...I saw a hat in my front yard last night."

"A red hat?" She paused. "You mean like the hat I found in the house after Marcus raped me?"

"Yeah. I think you're right about putting him on my list."

"You're losing your mind, Valentina. I'm telling you. I mean do you like your life? If you like your life stop this shit! You gonna be on that podcast telling niggas how you did too much if this blows up in your face. I see it for you."

Valentina glared at the floor of the train, her frustration building as Larisa continued to speak. "You know what, I don't care what you think at this point," she said, her voice rising. "I'ma do me regardless."

"Why even call me then? I mean, are you sure you not jealous that folks are moving on in their lives without you?"

She ended the call, still fuming.

Larisa didn't have to believe her. Besides, RoRo was her focus now and so she had to have a clear mind.

Valentina kept her eyes between RoRo and the window, watching as they passed through station after station.

As the train approached the next stop, Valentina saw him standing up to exit. She quickly gathered her things and made her way off the train, determined to find out what he was up to.

Following him closer than possible, she was shocked when her arm was grabbed, and she was shoved against a billboard encased in hard plastic.

It was her brother Nevin.

"Ouch! You hurting my arm."

"Get the fuck over here," he said, pushing her harder against the wall onto a sign for vaccinations. Then he observed her bruised face. "What happened to you...you look...bad. What–."

"I got my ass kicked! Now what you doing here?" Valentina yelled as she watched RoRo get away by looking around him. "How did you...how did you even know I was–."

"Larisa told me. I mean what you doing?"

She was betrayed once again. "I...he...it's too much to talk about. But I've been receiving text messages and I found a red hat on my lawn."

"A red hat?"

"You know what...I hate Larisa for doing this shit! She ain't have no business telling you."

"Before you get mad at her, just remember she's my fiancé'."

She giggled. "What nigga says fiancé' as much as you?"

"Why you following RoRo?" He said firmer. "Do you even know what you doing? First, it's Shug now it's RoRo?"

"She told you that too. Wow.'"

"It's like you won't stop until you ruin everybody's fucking life. Including your own. And I don't want that for you."

Valentina glared and pointed at him. "Ohhh...I get it now."

"Fuck you talking about?"

"You don't want me hanging with your precious *fiancé*." She giggled, pointing in his face. "Now I see what all this shit is about."

He looked down. "Valentina..."

"You think I'm bad news! Just say it!"

"You mean because you got my last girlfriend locked up for getting involved in one of your schemes?"

"It was that ho's idea to steal them tampons! She thought she could sell 'em for the low and get money because they was running out of cotton in the US due to–."

"You better not be getting Larisa involved in your shit."

"There it is..."

"Whatever this is, you can go at it on your own, Valentina. But leave my girl out of it."

"If I don't?"

"You don't want to fuck with me, Valentina."

"Wow. You think if I don't have her, I won't still do what I gotta do. Guess what, you wrong."

"Have I made myself clear?"

Silence.

He grabbed her coat and shoved her against the billboard again. "Have I made my fucking self clear or not?"

Several patrons stopped walking to see what was going on.

She took a deep breath. "Yes, little brother."

He released her. "Good...now go home."

"I got somewhere else to be and then–."

"Get back on that fucking train before I smack the shit out you!" He pointed behind her. "Now!"

Embarrassed and hurt, she walked toward the train just as it pulled up. Sitting down in the back, she was furious as she received another text message.

It's funny. In a little while you'll be locked up too. And I can't wait to see it.

CHAPTER NINE
SHARDS

TEXT: Your so-called friends are talking, dear. They spilling the beans on all your shit. Folks is tired of covering for you, and now you going to pay the price.

Valentina walked through the crowded casino floor in Baltimore, her long black hair flowing behind her. She made her way to the slots area where she knew RoRo would be.

After receiving that text message it was time to go harder and now, she wasn't sneaking around.

Before getting comfortable at the slot machine, she spotted him sitting not too far away at another. He was eagerly placing bet after bet. Brushing her hair behind her ear she walked over to him. "We gotta talk."

"What you doing here? And what happened to your face?"

Oh. She forgot about that.

"Nothing."

"You sure?" He frowned. "Because you look fucked up."

"How come you don't answer my calls, bruh?"

He glared. "You wildin' now. 'Cause I don't even know what the fuck you talking about?"

"I been hitting you for days with no answer. Luckily, I know about this gambling habit, or I would not have been able to catch you."

He grabbed her burned arm which was covered up by her coat. "You know what, let's get outta here cause you tripping hard now."

She snatched away due to the burned skin being sensitive to the touch. "Stop! That shit hurts!"

"What's wrong with your arm?"

"Nothing...I just–."

He grabbed her hand instead. "Well let's go."

She took a deep breath as he yanked her toward the exit.

Five minutes later they were sitting on benches on the side of the road. "Rowan, I–."

"Just because we grew up in that foster home together don't mean you get to call me by my real name." He paused. "And to answer your question, I feel like you want something from me I can't give."

"I need more!"

"You know what's weird as fuck right now?" He pointed at her with a shaking finger. "All my life I been trying to get you to see me. And now you can't stay off my phone? Make it make sense."

"You getting mad cause–"

"When we lived with Ms. Alexander, we were fucking with each other. But you said I was soft and started dealing with Milo. Then you dumped him and started going out with Jacob's crazy ass instead."

"So what's the problem?"

"Even though you ain't wanna be with me in public, you would still let me finger fuck under the covers. And I'm starting to think you like to collect hearts so you can own niggas."

"It wasn't just that. You were weird. Humpin' on a bitch's ass in the middle of the night. I wasn't with it." She paused. "But I'm looking out for you now as long as you keep all my secrets."

"Stop coming at me with all this shit!" He yelled, startling her. "I mean it!"

"RoRo, did you leave a phone at my house?"

"I don't know what you talking about."

"How come I don't believe you?"

"Since we asking questions, did you follow me a couple days back?"

Silence.

"Were you following me or not?"

"Why?" She lowered her gaze. "What was you up to?"

CHAPTER TEN
BLOODY RED

DECEMBER 10th

TEXT: You may have thought U covered your tracks, fish, but U left a breadcrumb trail. And it's coming straight to yo ass.

The text messages were getting more vicious... And mean...

Valentina sat in her cozy kitchen, the afternoon sun streaming through the window and warming her skin. Wanting some mint tea, she reached up to the cupboard above the sink and pulled out a small red teapot with yellow butterflies throughout. Trying to rush but also taking it easy, she filled it with water from the tap and placed it on the stove to boil.

As she waited for the pot to heat up, she moved over to the counter where her phone was charging. Device in hand, she opened her podcast app and selected the latest episode of *An Ugly Girl's Diary*.

After the intro was done, she listened to the guest. The woman, named Ericka, talked about where she was from and how appreciative she was to be on the show. Valentina wished she could be a guest too, especially after she solved her case.

As the water on the stove had begun to boil, Valentina walked back to it and turned off the heat. Glued onto every word, she reached into the cupboard again and pulled out a tea bag. Still locked in, she placed it in her favorite mug and poured the hot water over it, letting it steep. The aroma of the tea filled the air, calming and comforting her.

Afterwards Valentina took her mug and went to sit at her small table, while the podcast's narrator's voice continued to boom from the speaker. Totally enthralled, Valentina took a sip and leaned back in her chair, letting herself get lost in the girl's story.

And then she said, *"I started getting weird ass text messages. Oh, I'm sorry, can I say ass on your show?"*

Courtney giggled. *"Yes."*

"Okay, so I started getting these weird ass messages from someone who said I hurt them in life. And I didn't know who it was. Because I try hard to live my life good and not treat people like your boyfriend Tye. But these text messages led me

to believe someone was going to hurt me. Or ruin my life even though I was nice to most people."

The teacup fell from her hand, sending hot liquid splashing everywhere.

"Fuck!"

Valentina sighed as she surveyed the mess on her living room floor. The yellow teacup she had cherished for years lay in pieces, scattered in shards of broken ceramic. She couldn't believe she had been so careless, but the podcast continued to hold her attention.

"So, what types of things did the texter say?"

"You know, at first, they tried to lead me. Make me think I met them somewhere else. So we continued texting and then things got weird. Stuff in my life started getting out of control. And I don't know what to do."

"Okay, you do know what kind of podcast this is right? I help people who are tired of getting fucked over get back at those who did them wrong."

"Yeah, I know."

"So why come here? It sounds like you're the villain."

"I really am not. Trust me."

Courtney sighed. *"Okay, so why did you proceed with texting after it was clear you didn't know the person?"*

Valentina grabbed a broom and dustpan and began to sweep up the pieces, taking care not to cut her fingers on the sharp edges. She also made mental notes not to text the person back anymore. It wasn't like they were replying anyway.

"Ouch!" She screamed out. A piece of the mug had dug into the sole of her foot, causing blood to splatter everywhere. "Shit...shit...SHIT!"

The universe was kicking her ass.

She was fucked up in the face, her arm was burnt and now her foot was cut. She was falling down quickly. Sure she could have paused the podcast, but the woman was telling a version of her story she wanted to hear.

She wrapped her foot up in a cut up white towel and hobbled back to the mess. As she cleaned, bled, and listened, her mind drifted back to the memories associated with the mug. The countless mornings she had spent sipping tea from it at Ms. Alexander's house with Milo, Nevin, RoRo, Shug, and Pumpkin. Ms. Alexander had purchased one for them each as homecoming gifts, and as far as she knew she was the only one who still had hers.

Memories of the past fucked with her for a moment, and so she paused the episode.

Once the last shard had been swept up and disposed of, Valentina looked around her cleaned living room. With a final sigh, she put the broom and dustpan away and sat down on the couch. She decided to pour herself another cup when...

CRASH!

Valentina froze as she heard shattering glass coming from outside her front door. She quickly hobbled to the window, her heart racing with fear. To her horror, she saw that someone had smashed the windows of her Tesla, which was parked on the street instead of the garage.

"I know they didn't! I know they fucking didn't! What the fuck?" She yelled. "I told them somebody was out to get me!"

She quickly grabbed her phone and dialed 911, her hands shaking as she spoke to the operator. "Hello, I need some help! Somebody just bust my shit wide open!"

"Ma'am, I have no idea what you're talking about."

"I was drinking tea and someone broke my window! My car window."

"You have to calm down and give me more information."

Valentina explained more and gave them her address, her eyes still glued to the destruction of her ride outside.

As she waited for the police to arrive, she felt a mix of anger and vulnerability wash over her. She knew she was right about someone being out to get her. And now she didn't feel safe in her own home.

It seemed like forever, but when the police arrived, Valentina quickly explained what happened in great detail. They took her statement and looked for evidence, promising to do everything they could to catch the perpetrator.

Sure you will.

And then one of the officer's asked, "What happened to you?"

"I just told you! Somebody bust my shit up!"

He glared. "I mean with your face. Your arm. And your foot?"

She looked down at the trail of blood leaving her house. "Uh...nothing. I...you know...they um...people be–."

"Do you know who could be responsible for vandalizing your car?" He got tired of the run around and decided to lead the conversation.

Silence.

"Ma'am, do you know or not?"

She wanted to snitch or make something up. Surely this would be a good time to run Pumpkin, RoRo, and even Milo under the bus. But she had other plans for them.

"Ma'am, do you know or not?"

"Uh...no...I don't."

"Well, if we find out anything we'll let you know." He tore a piece of paper off and handed it to her before pulling off with his partner.

As she watched the police drive away, she knew that she needed to find a way to feel safe and secure again. She knew it wouldn't be easy, but she decided to call her aunt and leave a message.

"I know it's been a few weeks since I talked to you, but I need to see you. Someone is trying to ruin my life, auntie. Can I come over? Please."

CHAPTER ELEVEN
FUNKY FUTURE

DECEMBER 11th

TEXT: It's time to come clean, honey. Confess. It's the only move you can make while U still can.

Valentina stepped inside the psychic shop and her eyes were immediately drawn to the colorful crystals and tarot cards that were displayed on shelves lining the walls. The shop was dimly lit, but the light from a large crystal ball in the center of the room cast a warm glow on the space.

Soft R&B from the nineties filled the air and made Valentina feel at home.

As she stood in the lobby, a black woman with long, flowing gray hair sat behind a small table, her eyes closed in concentration. She was surrounded by candles and herbs, and she held a crystal pendulum in her hand.

As Valentina walked closer, still wanting to give the current customer her space, she could hear the soft murmur of the woman's voice as she spoke.

The customer who was getting a reading nodded eagerly, hanging on her every word.

The atmosphere in the shop was one of peace and tranquility, and Valentina couldn't help but feel a sense of calm wash over her as she browsed the items on the shelves. She picked up a small piece of amethyst, feeling its weight in her hand and admired its deep purple color.

When the customer left, the woman said, "Please sit. I'll be right with you."

Valentina sat nervously in the dimly lit room; her hands folded tightly in her lap. It had been a long time since she'd been to a psychic, and she felt desperate and willing to try anything to get answers.

Ever since the phone ended up on her bathroom floor, she had been plagued by nightmares and anxiety. Not to mention the red cap left on her lawn, Pumpkin and Shug beating her up, the burn on her arm and now a sliced foot.

The psychic took her seat across from Valentina and she couldn't get over her kind eyes and gentle voice. "I sense that you are trouble."

"Trouble?"

"Very much so."

Valentina nodded, her eyes filling with tears. "I did some things...I mean... someone that I trust is going to ruin my life," she said.

"How?"

"They know my deepest secret and they're going to use it against me."

The psychic closed her eyes and was silent for a moment. Then she spoke. "You are dancing with evil. And if you don't pause on what you're doing, you will suffer greatly."

"Can you elaborate?"

"The bruises on your face, on your arm and wherever else my eyes can't see are foreshadows of things to come. They are indicators that if you continue to go this way, you will be scarred mentally and physically for life."

"Oh...I..."

"But I also see a light, a protection trying to cut through. But you won't let it in. Do you have someone being overprotective of you?"

"No...parents passed away."

"Wow. I'm sorry to hear that." She sighed. "Well I sense that you've been carrying a heavy burden for a long time, one that you have not shared with many. It's time to do the right thing. Do you know what I'm speaking about?"

"I...I don't know."

"I think you do."

The voice in her mind said, *"Don't let her trap you."*

"Can I just get the reading?"

"Of course."

After the cards were laid, she said, "The next thing you do, will be the thing that changes your life for the worse. Don't do it. That is my only reading. That is my only warning."

The woman provided the service, but Valentina was too weighed down to appreciate the moment. And as she left the psychic's office, she realized that she was the only one who could control her life.

She was on her way to her car when her phone rang. She quickly answered but regretted it seconds later. "Hello."

"It's me!" Larisa said. "Don't hang up!"

"What you want?"

"I'm sorry. I really am about telling Nevin you were on that train. But you were acting crazy and–."

"Larisa, that was some foul ass shit and you know it!"

"Actually I don't remember you telling me not to tell him so it–."

"Is that what you wanna do right now?"

Larisa took a deep breath. "I'm sorry. I didn't think it would be a big deal. I didn't know you didn't want him to know."

"That's not the point. I trusted you and you betrayed that trust. Just like RoRo and Milo. And Pumpkin and Shug too."

"So have you found out anything to make you believe any of them are still involved with leaving that phone? Outside of the text messages on your personal cell."

Silence.

"Valentina?"

"Yeah...someone busted the car windows out of my car and broke into my window at home." It was a lie but she wanted it to sound more fantastic. "I cut my foot when they did."

"Did they take anything?"

"No."

"Oh...I see."

"So you still don't believe me?"

"I didn't say that. If you say it happened, I believe you. Plus I'm not gonna doubt you unless I get a reason."

"Why you calling?" She walked toward her car.
"Nevin said he didn't want you hitting me up no more."

"He said what?" She yelled.

"Told me not to get you involved. In all my mess."

"I can't believe he did that shit!"

"Yeah, right."

"I'm serious. I love your brother, but he knows the last thing he's supposed to be doing is getting in my fucking business. We have an understanding and he fucking that up." She breathed deeply. "Please don't say it. Just know that whatever you need I'm here. So what's the plan now?"

"I'm calling Jacob. I got another job for him to do."

"Oh no, Valentina. Noooo."

Pumpkin stood over the grill, flipping burgers and hot dogs with a pair of tongs. The cold winter air bit at her cheeks and nose but the smell of sizzling meat wafted through the atmosphere, making her belly growl with hunger.

Not only that, but the music was pumping hard with classic rap. She loved being around the hood element in Baltimore. She loved the sense of danger that always seemed to follow where there were women, weed and drink.

With her hands tucked in the pocket of her red bubble coat, she glanced around at the hustle and bustle of the neighborhood, watching as dark figures came and went from the surrounding homes.

So far no one caused an issue with her guests, so all was well in the hood.

As she tended to the food, she began to smell something else - a faint hint of smoke that seemed to be coming from the distance.

"You good, Pumpkin?" One of her guests asked as he pulled on weed.

"I smell smoke."

"You mean the smoke coming from the grill? Or this?" He raised the blunt. "Want a hit?"

She leaned in, took a pull, and shrugged, assuming it was just the grill creating some extra smoke in the air.

But as the minutes ticked by, the smell grew stronger and acrider. Suddenly, there was a loud crackling sound from inside her house where the windows fractured, and Pumpkin's heart sank as she realized what was happening.

"Oh my God," she whispered, dropping the tongs and running for the door. "What the fuck! That's coming from my house! Fire! Fire!" She rushed toward the blaze.

Yanking the door open she was met with a wall of flames. Heat and smoke billowed out, blinding and choking her. She could hear glass shattering and wood cracking as the fire consumed everything in its path.

"Help me! Somebody fucking help me!" She screamed.

She stumbled back, coughing and choking, as the inferno consumed her home. The flames licked at her skin, singeing her hair and clothes. This was a tragedy, and she could feel the heat searing her lungs, and she knew she had to get out before it was too late.

Suddenly four of her male friends grabbed her by the waist from behind and pulled her out. Any later and she would be dead. As they moved for the entrance, the house collapsed behind her.

When she reached the street, where she dropped on the curb, she coughed and sobbed. Her jeans were soak and wet as the snow and ice around melted from the intense heat of the blaze.

"Who did this shit?" She cried. "Who fucking did this shit?!"

As she lay on the ground, she could hear the sirens from the fire department in the distance. Her friends tried to console her, but it was of no use.

She lost her home.

She lost everything.

Regaining her breath, Pumpkin caught sight of a car pulling away from the scene. She squinted through the smoke and saw Jacob driving off.

Marcus left his apartment in Baltimore and slipped into his car feeling uneasy. But he shrugged it off and continued his way.

Besides, he was a street nigga and street niggas never felt safe.

Not really anyway.

The temperature was freezing as he walked past the row houses and the sound of chatter and laughter from the neighbors, the smell of fried food and the sound of cars passing by on the street. Sliding in his car, he glanced out his window and nodded at a few people he knew and still saw nothing suspicious.

Maybe I'm tripping. He thought.

He decided to stop at a gas station to fill up his tank. As he pumped gas into his car, he noticed a man lingering near the entrance to the convenience store. The man's gaze seemed to be fixed on Marcus, and he gave him a glare. But when the dude walked away, he headed inside to use the restroom.

He was washing his hands but when he heard the door to the bathroom open, he tensed up. Looking in the mirror he saw the same man from outside, now standing a few feet behind him.

It was Jacob and he had a smirk on his face.

"Fuck you want with me, nigga?" Marcus yelled.

Jacob, overpowering him with his height, yanked him closer like a rag doll. Turning him around, he grabbed him by the neck and stuck him on the other side of the throat with a needle.

Immediately Marcus felt high.

Like he had six shots of Henny back-to-back.

When he slithered on the floor, Jacob flipped him over. He pulled out his collapsible bat, snatched down his pants and rammed it up his anus. Marcus screamed out in pain, but Jacob didn't stop until he was bleeding and motionless.

When he was done he said, "You probably wanna know why I did this."

Marcus withered around, moaning.

"I saw on TV that you like to rape people, nigga." He said through clenched teeth. "So how does it feel?"

Jacob laughed, wiped the bat on Marcus' jeans, and walked out of the bathroom, leaving Marcus humiliated, squiggling and angry.

In agony and pain, he fixed his clothes, and called the police. Up until that point he never dialed 911 in his life. But the moment they came, one officer recognized him immediately and he regretted the shit. "You know what, never mind." Marcus said, leaning on his car, barely able to stand. "I'll be fine."

"What do you mean never mind? You said someone assaulted you. So what did they do?"

He was too embarrassed to tell the truth. "I said never mind. Leave it be!"

"I'm still gonna record this mess."

As he was talking to one officer, the other ran his information and looked at his partner when there was a hit. "We have a warrant for your arrest, Marcus. What you know about that?"

"A warrant for me? But I'm the victim!" He yelled, slapping his chest. "You hear me? I'm the fucking victim!"

"And you still will be…in jail." With that, he was taken into custody.

Sitting painfully in the backseat, the sound of sirens and police radios filled the air. He couldn't believe what was happening to him. Due to the narcotics they found on him at his court case years ago, he knew he would be incarcerated for at least three years.

In all the commotion, he had completely forgotten.

Valentina got him dead to rights.

Jacob met with Valentina in a dimly lit alleyway, the smell of garbage and stale cigarette smoke lingering in the air. The moment he showed his face, she handed him an envelope filled with cash. "That's for both jobs."

"I hear you," Jacob said, pocketing the money.

"Did you think about what I said? About giving us another try."

"Why would I be with a woman who thinks of ways to get people back like this?"

"What about you? You're the one pushing off."

"I was found in a sewer. Never had a family before you. So niggas expect the worse from me. But you...you had a chance and you fucked it up."

She looked down. "Jacob...I need you."

He frowned. "Are you using me as a weapon just to see me?"

Silence.

"Your face is still pretty. But nothing else changed. And until...you know what...it doesn't matter." He laughed and walked away.

CHAPTER TWELVE
PRETTY DIAMOND

DECEMBER 13th

TEXT: The evidence against you is mounting, Suga. I hope you like prison pussy because it will be served raw and unclean.

Valentina sat in the back of the salon, watching as Diamond sat in the stylist's chair in the front of the shop. Diamond's long, dark hair cascading down her back as the stylist put the finishing touches on it with expert precision.

With Pumpkin, Shug, and Marcus out the way she could dedicate more time to RoRo and Milo.

As Valentina hung in the background, she wished she was as happy as Diamond appeared to be, but it wasn't even close. Valentina couldn't help but feel a twinge of jealousy as she watched her laugh with Milo sitting next to her, with a proud look on his face.

They used to do that thing.

"So, what happened to you, pretty girl?" Valentina's hairdresser questioned.

"What difference does it make?" She snapped.

She was tired of everyone asking her like she was the most fucked up creature who ever crawled through Baltimore. At least six niggas in the shop were worst for the wear, including the stylist herself.

"Girl...I tried to ignore it until I noticed your arm." She paused. "But, anyway, what you think?" She shoved a mirror in her face, blocking her view. "You like it?"

Valentina tried to look around the mirror at Diamond and Milo who didn't see her. "Uh...yeah."

She shoved the purple mirror in her face again. "You didn't even look at it."

Valentina glanced at it quickly and then away from it to focus back on Diamond and Milo.

"You don't know me but if I don't get an honest answer about my work, it drives me insane. So I crave your opinion."

This bitch.

Valentina finally observed her own reflection, forced a smile, and said, "It looks great, Lani. I appreciate it."

"My name Batine."

"I mean Batine." Valentina quickly focused back on Diamond and Milo.

"You know them, don't you?" Batine asked.

"What you talking about now?"

She rolled her eyes. "You heard me."

"I mean, I know them kinda..."

"An ex-girlfriend?"

"Nah, he's about to marry that bitch. She's not an ex."

"I'm talking about you. Are you his ex-girlfriend?"

"Oh...no...just a friend. We grew up in foster care together. And recently he claimed he was getting married. I wanna see if it's true."

She nodded. "So what's your thing? Why so interested in them?"

"I just told you."

"You lying, but if you wanna waste time here, in my chair I don't mind. But you gotta talk to me too."

Valentina turned herself around and observed Batine. She figured she was the worst out of all the hairdressers or new. That would explain her station being way in the back, she should be lucky Valentina was sitting in her chair in the first place.

"Okay, how often are they here?" Valentina questioned.

She looked at Milo and Diamond. "You know what, this the first time I've ever seen him."

"How long have you been here?"

"At least a year."

Valentina glared. "Are you sure you've never seen them?"

"Yeah, because when she comes, she's always loud and shit. Want everybody to see her. But I've never seen his fine ass before in my life."

Valentina nodded. "Good."

"But I get the impression they love one another just observing them now. Maybe you should let 'em be. Instead of keeping my seat warm."

Just then another text message came through:

How does it feel to not be able to trust anyone? Enjoy your freedom. For now.

When she looked at Milo, he was texting on his phone and her heart dropped. She felt she had him now.

He was the one sending her messages.

Suddenly, everything was clear.

Valentina sat at a small table near the window of the cozy coffee shop. The warm glow of the setting sun filtered through the glass, casting a soft light on the patrons inside. The aroma of freshly brewed coffee filled her nose as she took a sip from her steaming mug.

While business was as usual, Valentina sat back in her chair, taking in the sights and sounds of the bustling shop, feeling content and at ease as she kept eyes on that bitch.

She texted Milo.

Valentina: **Can we talk?**

Milo: **I'm out of town.**

He was lying. She'd just seen him.

Valentina: **Out of town where?**

He didn't respond.

Valentina: **Remember that whatever happens next is because of you Milo.**

While she texted, she saw Diamond on the phone, laughing joyously with who she was sure was Milo. He couldn't text her back, but he had time for that bitch.

So when Diamond ended the call, Valentina got up and walked toward her. "Your hair is beautiful."

Diamond grinned and fingered it. "Really?"

Valentina pulled out a chair. "Yeah, who did it?"

"I got it done by this chick at the salon down the street."

"Charge much?"

"I don't know...I didn't pay for it." She looked upward and had a gaze in her eye. "My hair appointments are booked in advance. Way in advance by my fiancé'."

It took everything in her not to spit on her. "Whoever paid must really love you."

"Oh...that's one thing about my nigga. He is sooo good to me. Like...like I never met a person who sees me like he does."

"Really, he sounds like my boyfriend."

"Girl, if you have one percent of the man I got you doing good. I mean like really, really good."

"Why you say that?"

"The reason I love him so much is because he shelters me from shit that will hurt my feelings. Like, most people would be upset if you don't meet their family members and friends. But he refused to introduce me, you know. Because he want our shit to be good."

"Refuses?"

"Yeah...his mother, father, and everybody else are all fucked up. Like they don't care about him. He even called every friend he has dangerous and untrustworthy."

Valentina's jaw twitched. "Really?"

"Yep, he says–."

"I know you're excited about getting married, but has it ever occurred to you that he might be lying?"

She frowned.

"I don't mean no disrespect, but men do lie." Valentina said, putting a hand on her chest.

"I...I don't get why you would say something so mean. I don't–."

"I didn't mean to scare you."

"I'm not scared. I...I guess I don't know what you mean. Like, why did you even come over here?"

"You invited me to sit down."

Her mind quickly replayed the events leading up to her being insulted. "No I didn't! So why did you come over here? I...I was having a good day and then you…and then you sat over here and got goofy."

"Calm down, girl. You ain't dead." Valentina giggled. "I think we have someone in common anyway. Let me show you." Valentina pulled out her phone, scanned and pulled up a picture. When she had it, she handed it to her.

Her eyes widened as she viewed what was displayed on the screen. Despite crying, she continued to scroll until the pictures stopped being of the sexual positions Valentina had with Milo and of pictures of some unopened packages.

Sliding the phone angrily across the table she said, "Who are you?"

"Does it matter?"

Diamond wiped her tears away harshly. "What kind of person would do something like this?"

"Call me a saint. 'Cause I just saved your life."

OUTSIDE THE COFFEE SHOP

Clouds began to form in the sky as a steady stream of people walked up and down the sidewalk, some heading into the coffee shop, others leaving with steaming cups in hand. A line had formed outside, with customers patiently waiting to place their orders. At the curb, a few small tables and benches had been set up, and they were quickly filling with patrons eager to sit and enjoy their drinks in the cool air.

It was there that the stranger, the one who had been seen with RoRo, saw an altercation brewing inside. First, he saw Diamond crying into her palms as she bolted out of the doors. Then he saw Valentina who looked in the direction Diamond exited, a sneaky smile on her face.

Now it was time to make the proper introductions when she walked out.

"You a troublemaker." He said, stepping up to her. "Aren't you? And judging by the face and that limp, someone already let you know. Tell me something, who beat your ass?"

When she saw the man from the garage parking lot her knees got weak. "You following me?"

He tucked his hands into his jacket pocket. "You stepping to me about stalking? I mean, weren't you in that parking garage? Being nosey."

She was caught. "What do you want?"

"Did you get your car windows fixed?"

Her eyes grew larger. "You did that?"

"What you think." He bragged, touching his chest.

"What do you want?"

He seemed to move toward her quickly. Like he defied the laws of gravity. "Like I said, I saw you when you left the parking lot. And since that time I have been following you. So my question to you is this, what do *you* want?"

"With who?"

"RoRo. Or me."

"I have some questions for RoRo. But you...I don't even know who the fuck you are. Now please get out my face because I don't even know your name. You could be–."

"Call me Brian."

"Like RoRo's middle name?" She laughed. "You know what, fuck off, Brian!"

He grabbed her hand and dragged her toward the alley next door to the coffee shop. Now she was out of view of the public and he could do anything to her if he desired.

Sure she saw people across the way sitting alone, lost in thought, while others were chatting and laughing with friends at a deli. But she doubted anyone would care if he tucked her in his trunk.

"I said what do you want with me, Brian?"

"You don't know who I am, but I know who you are. Do you understand that before we go any further?"

Her breath quickened. "I guess."

"Bitch don't fuck with me. I can tell by your beauty and your lip game that you say shit you want without repercussion. The shit stops now."

She nodded. "I get it. I mean, yes."

"So when I ask you a question, I need you to tell me what the fuck I want to know. Because I can do many things to you. Things you won't be able to see in advance. Do you understand that?"

She sighed. "Yes."

"So, comprehending all that, why were you watching us in the parking garage?"

"I was following RoRo to see what he's doing. Because someone is trying to destroy my life and I need that to stop."

"You're done with him...today."

"Why?"

"I don't have to tell you that. But what I will say is that what I got going on is serious. And if you fuck that up, there will be problems. For you."

She swallowed. "Whatever is going on...does it have anything to do with me?"

The sun had taken its exit and suddenly thunder clapped at the sky. It began drizzling on both of them.

The stranger smiled seeing she was rattled. "Yes. Yes it does."

She didn't believe him.

He wasn't police.

But why didn't she feel relieved?

"And you better keep your fucking mouth closed about this little meeting. Because if you tell RoRo or anybody else, I'll be back."

CHAPTER THIRTEEN
CROWDED

DECEMBER 14th

TEXT: U got money ready for your prison books? Lol. If not U should.

Things were starting to get serious for Valentina.

Sitting in her car, she was trying to hold back tears. She needed help with this new nigga.

She needed Jacob.

Clutching the steering wheel, her hands shaking as she dialed Jacob's number. She was desperate to reach him, knowing that if she didn't, Brian would make shit bad for her. But he was getting tired of the phone calls...tired of the gore...tired of the violence.

If only she listened to her brother, she may not have been in this situation.

Now it was too late.

She had successfully grown enemies in her backyard.

His phone rang and rang, but there was no answer. And her heart began to race as she tried again and again, but nothing. She knew she had to find a way to reach him, but with every passing moment, her fear grew.

Just as she was about to give up hope, her phone rang and she quickly answered. It was his number.

"Jacob," she said, her voice trembling. "Thank God, I've been trying to reach you. I need your help again. This man named Brian is going to kill me, and I don't know what to do."

Silence.

"Please, Jacob," she begged. "You don't have to answer now but if you can help me there is even more money involved."

"Are you alive?" He asked calmly.

"Am I alive? Yes…how else would I be–"

"Did he hurt you?"

"No…but…"

"Then don't call again."

When she looked down at the cell, she saw he had hung up, without telling her what she needed to know. That he would be to the rescue like he'd been since they were teenagers.

Putting the phone down, she threw herself back in her seat and looked up at the ceiling.

"Girl, what you doing sitting in your car?" She heard someone call out.

Valentina wiped the tears away that fell down her cheeks to hear where the voice was coming from. "Huh?"

"I'm over here! In the window."

Valentina giggled, which had been the first time in a long time. Watching her aunt, who was a big woman but fly as fuck, look out of the window while sitting on the toilet did something to her in that moment.

Valentina grabbed the large bag on the passenger seat, her cane because the stitches on her foot were starting to break open, and eased out, activating the alarm in the process. "I was just thinking, auntie. That's all."

"Wait, what happened to your face? And why are you limping and using a cane?"

"I just got stitches in the bottom of my foot. Other than that...let it be."

"Say no more. You know I always help you work shit out anyway but if you wanna do it yourself, go off." She laughed just before the toilet flushed, causing Valentina to chuckle again.

An hour later Valentina was sitting on her aunt's bedroom floor eating fish and fries. While her aunt was propped on her bed which was covered in papers, magazines, and retail boxes.

Despite the junky bedroom, Jessie's home was laced in the best furnishings that could be found. Most of the things Valentina bought her just because.

The woman was spoiled.

Jessie had one quirk that Valentina hated, and it was that she never cleared her bed. In fact, instead of making up her mattress, she created a spot on the left of her California king where she could roll into each night without knocking things off.

After she finished eating she said, "Auntie, you really did that. Per usual. It was sooo good."

"Girl, hush. I was just cookin' something light."

She wiped her mouth with her napkin. "I'm serious. I really needed this meal. Although I don't see how you eat fried fish in your bedroom."

"It'll air out." She winked. "And anything to get you and Nevin to come by, that's what I'm willing to do. I ain't seen Pumpkin and Shug in a minute either. They okay?"

Silence.

Jessie took a deep breath, pushed her plate to the side which was mostly covered in remnants of the meal she didn't want. Then she grabbed the bag Valentina brought. "Well since you not in the talking mood, it's gift time." First, she removed a shirt. "Oh my goodness! This is beautiful! I didn't even think they made Gucci shirts in my size. You always keep me fly."

"Glad you feelin' it."

Next, she removed some black pants, some Chanel jewelry, and some perfume. In total the gifts she gave her aunt was valued at over $5,000.

"I'm gonna kill them at work tomorrow. They so jealous of my put together game they don't know what to do."

Valentina continued to grin until suddenly she broke into tears.

The cry was long, hard, and serious. It shocked her aunt so badly that she trembled and knocked the plate off the bed and onto the floor. She didn't bother cleaning it, instead she rushed to her side, grabbed her hand and led her to the bed. "What's wrong, sweet girl?"

"Auntie, I'm in trouble." She moved a magazine from up under her ass.

"In trouble for what?"

"I don't know and it's...its..." She broke down harder as she thought about the current condition of her life. And the warning the man gave about keeping his secret. "I don't have anybody in my corner right now. I'm all alone and this shit is killing me."

"What am I?" She frowned. "How can you be alone when I'm here?"

"You know what I mean."

"Actually I don't." She sighed. "Do you or don't you know you can depend on me for anything?" Her glare was intense as she waited on an answer.

"Yes, but—."

"But what?"

"You're older and it's different."

"Valentina, instead of doing all you can to hurt my feelings, how about you tell me why you feel the way you do."

Valentina breathed deeply. Just her aunt being there was enough to reassure her that she wasn't all on her own. "I can't tell you a lot because I want to keep you safe."

"Then tell me what you can to survive."

"I think my friends are going to get me locked up for some shit from the past."

Her aunt breathed deeper. "Are you still doing the things you think will get you in trouble now?" She pointed at her.

Valentina shook her head. "Not *the thing*. That was one and done."

"Alright, I don't need to hear no more." She waved the air.

Valentina nodded. "Can I stay the night? And you tell me a story?"

"Of course, sweetheart. Let's go to the living room." She rubbed her knees and pushed herself up. "And I'll make you some tea."

CHAPTER FOURTEEN
GRUDGES

DECEMBER 15th

TEXT: Still checking on your so-called friends? Because they checking up on you. Bitch you about to be behind bars.

The sun was glistening brightly through the windows as Valentina sat on her couch, her eyes glued to the screen of her phone as she scrolled through the text messages that for days had haunted her. The warm rays of sunlight spilled across her face and illuminated the room, casting a golden glow over everything.

Zeroing in on each word, her thumb moved effortlessly over the screen to the point of arousing pain.

The sound of birds chirping outside caught her attention and she paused, when she saw a car driving toward her house. Slowly she got up and walked closer to the window and placed the phone down.

It was Nevin, parking.

When he exited his car, she crossed her arms over her chest and leaned against the door frame. "Why you here?"

"It's a nice day." He set the car alarm. "You should be out enjoying the weather."

"What do you want, Nevin?" Her words were firmer. "Aunt Jessie called you? 'Cause I didn't."

"I want to talk. To my sister. Is that allowed?"

They were drinking sparkling red wine as they looked at one another. Neither spoke, which was more so because Valentina was angry than anything else.

"So you're going to ignore me all afternoon?"

"I done gave you wine, let you use my bathroom multiple times...so what's up?"

"What I want to say to you is I'm sorry I haven't given you enough attention lately. If you knew what I have been going through, then you would know why. I know you think I don't love you, but I do."

She shook her head. "Boyyyyy."

"I do." He placed a hand on her leg.

"You got a funny way of showing it."

"I see how you should feel that way but I got a life of my own. And just 'cause we don't see each other doesn't mean I'm being funny." He breathed deeply. "It's just that I don't want this thing to get you going again. Because for you to be afraid of storms, you don't have any problem causing them."

She sighed. "You can believe me or not but it won't change my mind."

"You mean like the time you were in elementary school and you thought your teacher was from another planet?"

She glared.

"Or the time you thought Pumpkin and Shug were bugging your phone because they remembered things you forgot you told them when we lived with Ms. Alexander?"

"I was drinking and suffered blackouts which–."

"Caused problems. Caused storms. For all of us. Don't you see the connection?"

She took a deep breath and sat her glass down. "But this is different."

"How? Because you still worrying about text messages on a phone? A phone that probably don't have nothing to do with you."

Silence.

A deep breath rolled through his lungs. "I talked to auntie. And she told me you are worried about–."

"I wish she hadn't done that."

"Well you know how she is about us. About you."

She sighed deeply. She wanted to tell him about the man named Brian, but she couldn't trust him to keep the secret. "Someone busted my car windows out the other day."

"What the fuck? Who was it?"

"You think I fucking know?"

"And you still believe that Milo or RoRo could be involved? Because I don't. We grew up with them. They solid."

"I hear you." She sighed. "But it could've been Pumpkin, Shug or the boy Marcus too."

"But Shug in jail remember?"

"She can still make moves."

"Valentina, you gotta remember that we're all friends. Think of the secrets we never breathed a word about. Even when times got rough. You making a big mistake by–."

"I don't need you here for real because I'm doing good. Like I said, Shug's in jail, so is Marcus and Pumpkin's house was burned down."

"B...b...burned down by who?" He said with wide eyes. "Not Jacob...please don't say you unleashed Jacob."

Silence.

"VALENTINA, NOOOOOOOO!!! FUCK ARE YOU DOING?"

"Like I said, I'm good."

"You have just started a shit storm and the worst part is, we won't know who gonna try and take you out when the shit clears." He shook his head.

"Get out, Nevin."

He frowned. "But we were–."

"Now!"

He took a deep breath and exhaled. "Call me if you need me."

"The only thing I need right now is for you to get the fuck out my house. That's it!"

He nodded, got up and left.

Jacob sat in Valentina's living room, on her sofa, legs spread apart, man style. He didn't say much these days, then again, he never did back in the day either.

"I told you not to call me. Why aren't you listening?"

She walked over to him. "Me and Nevin been fighting."

Silence.

"And...and I don't know what to do."

"Why am I here, Valentina?" He said in a low thunderous voice.

"Jacob...I..." she drew in a long breath. "The sooner you realize that monster or not, I'm the woman you really love, the sooner you'll be able to smile again." She walked closer and sat next to him. "And don't you, don't you wanna smile again, baby? Don't you miss me?"

He got up. "I'm waiting on you to do the right thing...until that happens, I won't ever fuck with you again."

"But you can fuck me though, huh?"

"There's a difference. You don't know that by now?" He walked out.

Still upset with Jacob, Valentina stood in front of her full-length mirror, wearing a red satin robe as she brushed her long, dark hair. For a moment, she paused to take in her reflection, noting the tired lines around her eyes, the healing bruises on her lip and eye and the slight droop of her shoulders.

It was crazy that although she was considered beautiful, she was mostly alone.

Larisa had Nevin.

Milo had his fiancé'.

RoRo had his life and the stranger which seemed to occupy him all day.

But what about her?

The one man she cared for couldn't forgive the past.

Inhaling deeply, she walked over to her dresser and removed her jewelry, placing each piece carefully in its designated spot. Next, she headed to her closet to grab her pajamas. Slipping into her silver gown she made her way to her bed, and she couldn't help but think about the events of the day.

The text messages to her personal phone had gotten meaner. Not only that, but she also still hadn't managed to break the cryptic messages in the cheap phone.

Suddenly she remembered something about the phone. A detail she missed before. To get the answers she wanted, she had to get in contact with someone who probably didn't want to hear from her.

And yet, the feeling was mutual.

Valentina bustled around her kitchen, making a late-night snack for Milo.

Turned out he knew what happened with her and Diamond and it was his plan to cut her off for good. So when she called him and said she wanted to talk, he was irritated but she knew him well enough to know what would work.

Food.

"Come over for what?" He yawned.

"I need to talk to you."

"About fucking what, Valentina? Stop playing games and get to it."

She rolled her eyes. "First off, I know you mad. And I feel like you want to say more about that situation at the coffee shop with old girl. And I want to let you know that whatever you say to me, I can handle it."

"You wild. Soundin' like somebody did something to you."

"I'm just saying."

Silence.

"Milo?"

"I'm on the way. But I'm hungry too."

That was all it took.

Wearing her favorite yellow and black oversized sweater and a pair of faded jeans, her hair was pulled back in a messy bun. The warm light from the overhead fixtures casted a cozy glimmer over the kitchen.

Valentina started by taking out the ingredients she needed from the fridge and pantry to feed his ass. They had many late-night food raids over their time of being friends, so she knew what would work.

She decided to make a batch of homemade guacamole and some fresh tortilla chips. As quickly as possible, she cut avocados in half, removed the pits, and scooped out the flesh of the fruit into a mixing bowl. She added a squeeze of lime juice, some chopped tomatoes, onions, cilantro and a pinch of salt and pepper. Next, she mashed everything together with a fork until it reached the desired consistency.

This was like therapy, so every detail got her attention.

When she was done, she turned her focus toward the chips. Taking a package of corn tortillas she cut them into wedges. When she was done, she placed them on a baking sheet, drizzled them with a little olive oil, and seasoned them with salt.

Finally she slid them into the oven to bake just as she heard a knock on the door. She met with Milo more times than a little but why did she feel uneasy now? Wiping her hands on a red and white towel, she rushed to the door and opened it wide.

Milo was so fucking handsome, and she didn't understand why she never noticed until much later in life. I guess it was true what they said.

A taken man is a dick you can't resist.

"Hey."

"Hey." He said dryly, raising a bottle of wine. "Brought your favorite."

She smiled and opened the door wider as he walked inside. "I hope you're hungry," she said nervously.

"I said I was before I got here, right?" He was rude and snappy, but she didn't care if he would finally be honest.

She guided him to the kitchen table and placed down the chips and guacamole in the center. For fifteen minutes they both sat down and dug in, in silence.

When he slowed down eating, she said, "Ready to talk?"

"Can you give me five minutes? Fuck."

She nodded, stood up and moved toward the sink. To keep herself busy and to prevent herself from smacking him, she washed the dishes and tidied up. Her back may have been toward him, but she felt his rage.

"Why did you step to that girl at the coffee shop?" He asked.

Here we go.

She wiped her hands on her towel. "I'm sorry 'bout that."

"That's all you can say?"

167

"I don't know what else to give." She shrugged. "You know how I am when it comes to my family. I'm very overprotective and I wanted to meet your fiancé'."

"And you still haven't because that's not her."

She frowned. "W...what?"

"That was my cousin! And she was getting ready for her bridal shower because she's getting married this weekend."

She walked toward him. Covering her mouth she said, "Oh my God, I'm...I'm so sorry."

"I know you are. You always sorry."

She moved slowly toward the table, pulled out the chair and sat in front of him. "If she's not your fiancé', then who you marrying? Because...because I'm so confused right now."

"You want it straight up?"

"Yes."

"I been fucking Larisa for a while. Six months. And we serious."

Valentina's body seemed to droop downward. She didn't know what she was expecting, but it definitely wasn't that. "You...you what?"

"Like I said, we been dealing with each other for a while."

"This...you gotta be lying."

"I'm not. And I felt you wanting to trap me into telling you. By following me and shit like that, but it wasn't the right time." He shrugged. "I mean, I don't know how you knew, but you were right."

The breath seemed to escape from her lungs, but her chest still hurt. "I didn't know you were fucking Larisa. I hit you up tonight to ask you about the phone at my party. I was drunk so it didn't come to me until now."

"A phone?"

"Yeah...I found a phone in the bathroom the day after my party. And I remembered you raising something up in the air when I was on the patio with Nevin. And–."

"Oh yeah, it was a burner phone. Didn't know who it belonged to, and I thought...well...it doesn't matter. I just put it back in the bathroom where I found it." He paused. "I know it ain't right. But me and Larisa care about each other and–."

"You love her? After only six months."

"You know we been knowing each other for years. It's just –"

"You fucking foul!" She threw the towel in his face. "Nigga, I could go off right now! If Jacob was here, I'd..."

He looked at her. "Listen, I'm sorry you got upset over a phone, although I don't know why. But I'm feeling that girl. And what we got is real."

She got up and walked toward the sink. She saw a rind from an avocado and she was mad she cooked for his ass. "Why the lies?"

"Because I know you couldn't handle it. I mean look what you did to my cousin. And I know you can't forgive me right now...but I'm asking you to."

She turned around. "You don't deserve my forgiveness. Just get out."

He stood up and walked toward her. Quickly she removed a knife from the holder and aimed. "Don't make me slice you open!"

He raised his hands, backed away and walked out.

After taking a shower and oiling up her body, Valentina jumped in her car to pick up her prescription from the pharmacy. It was easier than it should have been for her to get Percocet's, and she was grateful because she had run out.

Besides, she had to confront somebody about what she learned, and she needed to be in the right frame of mind. And pills were how she did it.

Pulling back up at her house, she was shocked when she saw her front window busted open.

"Wait a minute!"

Parking any kind of way, she leapt out and ran inside her home. As she searched quickly with her eyes, she didn't see anything out of place. Her televisions were still on the wall.

Her laptop was still in her studio.

"What the fuck did they take?" She said to herself. "I mean, what could be more important than this shit?"

And then it dawned on her.

Slowly she walked to the back of her room.

The burner cell phone was gone.

But what the thief didn't know was that she transferred the text messages to a black and white composition book, where she had been trying to crack the code for the longest on paper.

So stolen phone or not, she would get the answers she needed.

CHAPTER FIFTEEN
WEALTHY ADDRESSES

Larisa sat at her desk; headset pressed to her ear as she took calls at Anavil Retail Store. They sold expensive appliances to business customers and smaller clients.

She hated the job, and everyone knew it, but it paid the bills. Plus every time she tried to leave, they would give her a penny raise to keep her in place but not enough to get out of the hood.

And so she never left.

Besides, the job had other benefits that she shared with Valentina, which increased her income, porch pirating.

Tired, Larisa rubbed her temples, trying to stifle a yawn. Her eyes were blurry, and her voice was low and monotone, indicating she was exhausted. Taking phone calls at work, it was clear that she was struggling to stay focused. But despite her best efforts, she kept drifting off, missing key pieces of information each customer would provide.

And then, "Larisa, you better get your little friend because I'm not playing with her ass."

Her eyes flew open to see her co-worker with a mustard stain on her shirt hanging over her head. "What you talking about?"

"Your fucking friend. She downstairs in the lobby getting on everybody's nerves."

"What's her name?"

"I don't know. She got bone-straight hair. Looks like she mixed with something but mainly she just thinks she's cuter than everybody else. And she's mad."

Just at that moment her phone rang, and she saw it was Milo.

"Girl, what you gonna do?" Her co-worker said, slapping her hand. "Because we got a poll on who 'bout to stomp the bitch."

"Oh...tell her I'll be down in a moment."

"Hurry up before I kick her ass." She stormed away, shoes click-clacking in the process.

Larisa grabbed her cell phone, walked into the bathroom and then a stall. "What's going on, baby? You know I'm at–"

"She knows."

Her eyes widened. "What? How?"

"I told her last night."

She placed a free hand on her belly. "Why would you do that shit?" Her eyes widen. "It doesn't make any sense."

"Trust me, I didn't want to. I wasn't even trying to make this call, but I feel like you should know."

"When did this happen?"

"Last night."

She rolled her eyes. "Now everything is gonna blow up in my face."

"I know you didn't want to tell Nevin about us, but maybe it's time. You gotta let everybody know what's good."

"You ruined everything."

"Ruined what? Us finally making it official? To be happy. I fucking want you, girl. What you trying to tell me? You don't want me?"

"Of course I do!"

"Then why you care? This is a way for you to be free. You can't possibly tell me you not relieved."

"I gotta go, Milo."

"Larisa, just–."

She hung up.

Standing in front of the bathroom mirror, her eyes fixed on her reflection. This secret was foul on many levels and would start more drama than she felt like dealing with.

And then there was Valentina.

Who could be vicious.

Violent.

Dangerous.

Larisa tried to hold back tears while her lips pressed tightly together. The longer she stayed in place, her eyes reddened, and her mascara smudged, indicating that she would be no good. "Okay, Larisa...it's time to get it over with."

Grabbing a few tissue papers, she smeared the tears away, tossed them in the trash and stormed out the bathroom.

It took some time, but Larisa finally made her way through the crowded lobby of her busy building, her eyes scanned the sea of faces as she searched for Valentina. Moving slowly, she weaved her way through the throngs of people, her head turned left and right quickly. Larisa's expression was determined and when she didn't see her, she sent a text.

Where R U

Looking up again, she saw some people were on their phones, some were deep in conversation. Searching the crowd, she finally saw Valentina standing in the middle, while others walked around her hurriedly.

Valentina remained still.

Her heart going wild in her chest, Larisa's bop slowed a little as she approached.

Valentina's chest rose and fell.

Standing in front of her, Larisa said, "Hey."

"First things first, did you break into my house and steal that phone? Because it won't work. I still got the messages recorded on paper."

"Fuck are you talking about? I ain't break into your shit."

Valentina glared. She believed her as far as that was concerned.

"What's up?"

"You really wanna do this shit in front of your co-workers?"

She looked at the busy lobby and swallowed the lump in her throat. "No...uh...let's go outside."

Valentina hit an "about face" like she was in the military. Walking quickly out the door and toward the middle of the parking lot. After a minute she stopped next to her white Tesla.

"Got the window fixed?" Larisa said making bad small talk. "That's good."

Silence.

"Um...what is it, Valentina?"

"You know what it is, bitch."

"I...I–."

"You fucked Milo."

She looked down. "It's bigger than that."

"Did you fuck him or not?"

"Yeah but..."

"So you a slut?"

Larisa trembled with rage. Because as much dick as Valentina licked, she didn't feel like there was any room. "Hold up now. I'm not gonna let you talk to me any kind of way. I feel as though–."

SMACK!

Valentina hit her on the left side of the face. And when she turned her head the other way she smacked her again.

Larisa placed her hands on both sides of her cheeks. "Valentina, I let you get that off because–."

"You know Milo was my every now and again! And you took that from me!"

"Why you so mad? It's not like you still fucking him. It's been months."

"Bitch, I fucked him the night of my party!"

Her eyes widened. Her heart broke. "No...no you didn't."

"You acted like you loved my brother! I knew in my heart something was off but had no idea I would find out that my best friend and my brother's fiancé would stoop so low. You probably the one sending me those messages."

Larisa continued to cry hard. "Like I said, I don't know what you talking about. I'm not sending you any messages."

"I can't believe this shit." She looked on the ground as if searching for answers. "Everybody around me foul."

"I know you upset, Valentina. And I get that. But a lot is going on that you don't know about. And if I could tell you I would."

"This is going to destroy my brother," Valentina said to herself. "And for you, I ain't got no more words."

Valentina jumped in her car, backed up, almost running over her work kitten heels as she pulled off.

When she was out of view, Larisa dug in her pocket and removed her cell phone. "So you still fucking, Valentina?"

"No...I mean just one time. But it's–."

"It's over! Die slow, bitch!"

CHAPTER SIXTEEN
CRINGE

DECEMBER 16th

TEXT: You thought you were untouchable, but justice always finds a way. Your lil luxurious lifestyle is bout to come to a crashing halt.

Valentina was driving as memories of the argument with Larisa flooded her mind, each one causing a fresh wave of pain. On her way home, she couldn't shake the feeling that at some point she would have to tell Nevin.

But could he handle it?

After parking the car, she walked into her home, closing the door behind her. She tossed her purse on the small table in the foyer and made her way towards the living room.

As she turned the corner, she froze in shock.

There, sitting on her beloved recliner, was Brian's creepy ass.

As he stared at her, his eyes were menacing. He was dressed in all black and his legs were crossed as he remained silent. Valentina's heart began to race as she realized that her life could be over by the end of the night.

"What...what are you doing here? How did you get in?" She demanded, her voice shaking.

Slowly she started pointing at him. "It's you...you stole the phone? You sent the text messages?"

"Fuck you talking 'bout?" The stranger stood up, towering over her. "Did you tell people about me?"

Maybe it wasn't him.

"No...I...I didn't."

"I don't believe you." He glared.

"I promise to God I didn't. I was too afraid you would hurt my family. I haven't spoken to RoRo, and I haven't even seen him."

"Good, because I'm here to collect on a debt," he growled, his voice deep and menacing.

"A debt! For what? RoRo?"

"Nah, this is more about you than anything else." He pointed at her. "I've done some research and asked around about you. It took me a while, but I met a Pumpkin. And what she said was very revealing and I got the impression she's after you. So be careful." He paused. "Anyway, it seems you've taken a lot of things from a lot of people, and it's time to pay up."

Now she understood.

It was about porch pirating.

She thought it was something else.

Walking away, she flopped on her sofa. "So this was always about me?"

"Not really. But when you followed RoRo, you left the door open to your own backyard. And now I see a pay day." He looked around. "After all, look at how you living. I want a piece of this lifestyle too. Can you blame me?"

"What's your business with RoRo? Since you blackmailing me you might as well tell me the truth."

"Nah. I'm good. I like secrets."

Valentina's mind raced as she tried to think of a way out of this situation. She knew things would come back on her soon, but she didn't know how.

"How much?"

"$5,000."

She wanted to throw up.

"I...I don't have any money," Valentina stammered. It was the truth. She had been paying Jacob so much cash she was broke.

"Too bad." He reached into his pocket and removed a gun. "Maybe I'll just kill you now and–."

"No! I said I don't have any money. But I can make a few moves if you give me some time."

The stranger glared. "Let me say it again, I don't want you to talk to your brother. Or RoRo."

"Wait...why you mentioning my brother?"

"You heard me right? This stays between us. I want you to use that pretty little mind of yours and think of a better way to get me my paper." He stepped closer to her, leaned down and grabbed her arm.

"I'll think of something." She sniffled. "But...but what if I can't?"

"Then I hope you got a life insurance policy on Nevin, because either way I'ma get paid."

Valentina sat in the tub, letting the warm water soothe her aching body. Tears streamed down her face as she thought about her current situation. She had limited money in the bank, true, but she didn't have enough liquid assets to pay out five thousand dollars.

Growing up, Valentina had always dreamed of making something of herself, of escaping the poverty and violence that plagued her neighborhood when she was in foster care. And she called herself doing just that when she started snatching packages.

Now she realized she was the brokest person she knew.

A Tesla sat outside.

She had every designer label known to man.

And yet when her life depended on it, she didn't have enough money to save it.

Her cooch didn't even have a value because she didn't have a nigga on the side to earn.

Valentina let out a sigh as she reached for the bar of soap on the edge of the tub. Washing her body she tried to think of a plan. Because if she knew one thing, it was that the man didn't care for her tears.

As she dried herself off and got dressed, an idea came to mind.

CHAPTER SEVENTEEN
RUN

DECEMBER 17th

TEXT: I saw your friends at the police station. They telling everyone. And soon the whole world will know.

Valentina sat on the front porch of her aunt's house, staring blankly at the bags of food her aunt was unpacking. It was one of those sneaky warm days in the winter that folks brought out their motorcycles, picnic tables and grills for. And her aunt Jessie was no exception and so she planned a Christmas style Barbecue.

But she couldn't enjoy herself. That last text message about the police station almost took her out, and she tried to put it out of mind.

"Valentina!"

Valentina was in her own mind and unaware she was being summoned.

"Come on, Valentina," her aunt said, noticing her niece's somber expression. "People gonna be here soon. And we gotta get shit set up so folks can eat. Because you don't want my friends coming over this bitch without at least a snack on the table."

Valentina forced a smile and got up from the step. When they were in the backyard, she helped her aunt unfold tables and lay them out on the lawn. Together, they arranged the sandwiches, fruit, and drinks.

As they worked, Valentina's aunt told stories of her mother, reminiscing about the good times they shared and the memories they made. Valentina couldn't help but smile, feeling a small sense of comfort in the familiar tales.

Besides, she didn't have one single memory outside of the ones her aunt told her about her parents.

But for her it was good enough.

An hour later, people started piling in and to be honest, Valentina was relieved that she wouldn't have to sit with her aunt alone. Besides, she had other things on her mind.

The sun was just beginning to set, casting a warm golden glow over the breezy but comfortable day. Every now and again Valentina's aunt looked over at her and eventually made her way to her space. With a small smile, she squeezed her hand tightly. "You wanna tell me what's up?" She fanned a fly. "Because I can't do this quiet game with you right now."

"I found out something." She closed her jacket to combat the small chill.

"You and these cryptic messages."

"I know...and I understand why it seems annoying, but that phone has led to so many things. Stuff I should know."

People laughed in the background as they ate, talked shit, and enjoyed cool cans of beer and desserts. Valentina wished she could mentally join them, but she was somewhere else.

"Talk to me, niece."

"Nevin's fiancé is cheating."

She leaned back. "Chea...cheating? For real?"

"Yes."

She looked down. "Oh...I..." the words seemed to disappear.

"I know how you feel, auntie. I feel the same way."

"But she's such a nice girl."

"She's one of my best friends. But she ain't hardly nice. At least not as nice as I thought she was."

Her aunt took a deep breath. "Damn I wish these young people could keep it loyal. What is so fascinating about having more than one person in and out your bed? I just don't get it." She fanned the fly away again. "What's your plan?"

"Don't know." She shrugged.

"You gotta know something."

"Auntie, I'm 100 percent sure I don't know shit. About anything. Since I found that phone my world has been turned upside down."

Her aunt nodded. "Okay, let's work it out. How serious is the situation? With Nevin?"

"She's in love with someone else."

"What the fuck! This ain't making sense if she was supposed to be marrying my nephew."

"Jessie, can you tell me where the extra chicken is?" Her friend with a sweat stained neckline asked, walking up to them. "You ain't put enough out and we still got room for more. Shit, if I had known you would've—."

"Girl, the extra chicken is at your house. Where you left the meal you were supposed to bring for the fifth time. Now don't start with me."

"You ain't have to go there," she mumbled as she walked away.

"That was mean," Valentina giggled.

"Fuck that. My niece and nephew got an issue. I could care less about Carla's gut." She took a deep breath. "How you feel about all this?"

"I feel like this will destroy my brother. At the same time I don't know if he can do better than her. I mean you seen the kind of women he used to deal with. Rough broads. The kind that look like they can lift cars. Shit, I heard a few of them were dating other chicks now. But Larisa is classy. More right for him if that makes sense."

"That's a little harsh."

"We lie to each other now?"

She took a deep breath. "Nah, I definitely don't want to create that narrative." She placed two fists on her hips. "So I guess you found out from Larisa."

"No."

She lowered her head. "How then?"

"Well, to keep it short it was Milo."

"Milo?" Her eyes widened. "How did he get in the picture?"

Silence.

Her aunt sat back slowly. "You got to be kidding me. Larisa going in for Milo? She's too tall for him."

"Auntie, I already went through these phases. From the why's to the when's. Now I need access to your mind."

"Like you said, you already heard all this. But it's new to me. Give me a few minutes to process this mess."

She sighed. "Waiting."

Her aunt was quiet, looking up...and then down. "Okay, I think you should tell him."

"Really?"

"Yeah."

"But it will ruin—."

"I know you already said it, but I'll say it again." She waved the air. "I been married ten times. And every time I stayed in the situation longer than I should have. And if somebody, anybody could have saved me the drama of the years I wasted, would have been much obliged."

Valentina nodded. "You're right."

"She's your friend but—."

"He's my brother," she whispered to herself. "So he trumps her."

"Exactly. And if anybody got a problem, even Larisa, tell her it's family over everything. That's how I feel. And let her bald-headed ass sort it out."

"You know she looks cute with that cut."

"You ain't lying. She fine as silk." She chuckled. "I'm just too mad to give her more right now."

They laughed, both of their shoulders knocking into each other.

CHAPTER EIGHTEEN
JEALOUS THINGS

DECEMBER 19th
TEXT: Are you still out of jail? I'm asking for a friend.

With everything going on Valentina forgot she still owed money to the blackmailer. And it was time to get a little help.

Hopeful, Valentina strutted into the bank, her designer heels clicking against the marble floor. She was dressed in a red Gucci blazer and carrying a black Louis Vuitton handbag, her long hair styled in loose waves that cascaded down her back like waterfalls. She had always been one to flaunt her wealth and success, but today she applied more pressure.

Confident as fuck, she approached the loan officer's desk and flashed a steady smile. She had all her paperwork in order and had even dressed in her best outfit to make a good impression.

When Valentina was comfortably seated the woman said, "Ms. Cash, I understand you want *cash.*"

"I actually need it," she giggled cutely.

"Most people do if they come see us so I'm sure you do. How much?"

"How much? I told them that already, isn't it on the application?"

"Well, I'm asking again."

She swallowed the lump in her throat.

Maybe dressing too fly was a bad idea after all. "I want or need $5,000."

"$5,000 huh? Chump change."

Silence.

"This doesn't look..." the loan officer's voice began to drift off as she scanned the documents. "This doesn't look too good for you."

At first Valentina was confident, but as she sat across from the loan officer, her insecurity began to flap like a loose dick. The woman behind the desk looked over her application with a stern expression, her eyes scanning over the numbers and figures as if she were reading all her dirty secrets.

"I'm sorry, Ms. Cash. But this doesn't give."

Valentina frowned. "Doesn't give?"

"No."

"Can you be professional at least?"

"I thought I was."

"Not really if you quoting Rolling Ray."

She folded her hands in front of her on the table again. "It's like this, at the end of the day, we can't approve your loan. Your credit score is too low, and you don't have enough assets. I mean, did you really think this would fly?"

Silence.

"Ms. Cash. I asked you a question."

"Actually I did."

"Well it won't. Not on my watch anyway. And not at my bank." She clasped her hands in front of her, fingers pointed Valentina's way like they were a loaded gun.

"How come I feel like something else is on your mind?"

"Nah...it's not."

"You sure? Because you acting like this your money or something."

"Well I do have shares in this company."

"But it ain't your bank."

The loan officer rolled her eyes and Valentina could tell the truth was on the tip of her tongue and she wanted to get it off.

"I mean, are you jealous of me or something?" Valentina continued.

"The thing I don't like is how you YouTubers think just because you got some followers, that it will automatically translate to dollars."

Valentina took a deep breath.

"Well that ain't how it works."

"So you follow my channel?"

"I mean I know who you are."

"If you know who I am then you know I'm about that life. Just because I'm not liquid—."

"Liquid? You not even frozen, for real, for real. You got some cars, some purses and shit like that, but you got less than five hundred dollars in checking and no savings account that we can see. Your house not even your property."

"It's rent to *own*."

"But it's still *rent*."

"Okay, I'll be honest. If I had it all figured out, I wouldn't be here. But it's like you don't even wanna give a nigga a chance."

"This is a professional institution."

"Exactly! And there are rules." Valentina shook her head. "You know what, I didn't come here for all of this. What's the bottom line?"

"You will not be approved." She said, her lips pressing together at the end, like she was preparing to give her a hard kiss.

"Wow."

"Maybe you can sell some of them purses you be flashing online. How about that."

Valentina felt like the wind had been knocked out of her. All her plans were being dashed because of a stupid credit score. "Okay, I know you don't like me."

"I ain't say all that."

"Girl, you don't like me. Let's keep it real since you got so much to say."

Silence.

"I just wanna know if there is anything I can do to get approved. Because somebody is out for my life."

Valentina was trying to keep the desperation out of her voice. Any other time she would've gone off, maybe even sent Jacob her way. But Jacob hadn't returned her calls since he'd last been at her house, and she needed cash.

The loan officer shook her head. "I'm afraid not. You'll need to work on improving your credit and saving more paper before you apply again. In the far...far future."

"How far?"

"When your tits and ass start to droop. Maybe that will be enough time."

"Wow."

The woman laughed.

"You have got to be the rudest bitch I ever met in my life."

"Maybe that's just what you need, Valentina. Or deserve. I don't know how karma is working for you but if your life looking like this, "she eyed her paperwork. "I'll say it's bad."

Valentina stood up, snatched her shit, pushed the seat back and stormed out. Embarrassed, she left the bank feeling defeated and frustrated. She had worked so hard to get to this point, and now she realized it was fake.

Standing in front of the bank her phone rang. She removed it from her pocket and answered. "Hello."

"How you doing, pretty lady?"

It was Brian.

"So you got my number, too? How?"

"Don't worry about how I got your number. Worry about how you gonna get me my money. Because I'm gonna see about you soon. I mean real soon."

When the call ended, she knew exactly what she had to do.

CHAPTER NINETEEN
GIVE IT

Larisa stood in her father's dimly lit tool shed, surrounded by dust and cobwebs. The musty smell of old wood and rust filled her nostrils as she searched for the wrench she needed to fix her car which started acting an ass right before she had to go to work.

She was still searching when she heard the door creak open and turned to see Valentina standing in the doorway, a serious look on her face. "Hey you."

"How did you know I was here?"

"You come here a few times a week. Your father told me you were back here."

"Well what do you want? The last time I saw you, you smacked me, twice."

She walked closer. "Larisa, I need a favor." Valentina's voice was low.

"Uh...huh." Larisa raised an eyebrow. "What kind?"

She hesitated for a moment before replying, "I need you to help me the way you used to. And I wouldn't be asking if I didn't need the money."

"Girl...you can't be serious. I thought you said you were done because of the police following you?"

"It's not police. It's worse."

"Well since we not good no more, I need my job more than ever. So the answer is no." She paused. "I mean why should I help you anyway?" She crossed her arms over her chest.

"Because with what's going on in my life right now, I can't do it alone."

Larisa put down the wrench and wiped her hands on her jeans. Next, she folded her arms over her chest. "I don't wanna be a part of this no more. I'm done with the porch pirating shit because it got my nerves too riled up. You been tripping so hard lately I'm starting to think people are following me."

"Well, might as well make some money one last time. Don't worry, I'll give you a cut of the addresses and any cut from packages I see on the way."

"You doing it alone?"

"Unless you going with me."

Larisa sighed. "Nah."

Valentina looked around the shed before lowering her voice. "Well, then I guess I'm going alone. I can't ask anyone else because they can't be trusted. It started with you and me, and it will end with you and me."

Larisa's heart began to race. "Valentina, shit is getting dangerous now. Are you sure, sure?"

Valentina's expression was determined. "I know the risks, but I need them addresses. Will you help me or not?"

Larisa took a deep breath and nodded. "What about Nevin?"

"What about him?"

"Does he know about Milo?"

"If he did, don't you think you would know too?"

Larisa sighed.

"Is it over?" Valentina asked. "Between y'all?"

"For now...since I found out y'all fucked." She shook her head. "But I gotta be honest, I miss that nigga. And we were saving the money I was getting working with you to get a place of our own. But...I feel like I ain't got no plans for my future no more."

That angered her. She would have to tell her brother now. They were making plans. "I hear you."

Larisa sighed. "Okay, I'll help you."

CHAPTER TWENTY
CRACKED

DECEMBER 20th

TEXT: Can I have your purses and shoes when shit comes crashing down?

After getting the addresses from Larisa with the biggest orders, Valentina sat in her living room, the latest rap music blasting through her speakers. She would go tomorrow. To pass time, she had been trying to crack the code of the secret text messages for weeks, and she was determined to figure shit out.

She was becoming obsessed.

As she scanned through the coded messages in her composition book, her eyes went over the strings of letters and numbers. She had tried every decryption method she could think of, but nothing seemed to work.

Just as she was about to give up, she remembered her favorite numbers and letters puzzle. It made her think of a specific code-breaking technique. She quickly grabbed a pen and paper and began to work out the method, her mind racing with excitement.

The message read:

aye wol vue

gap try her

ise fon

fwg wrh dop rne age

ffp ill pat bpm dpj kel yry

As the song came to an end, Valentina yelled.

"I fucking got it!"

Grabbing a clean sheet of paper she wrote the words again, this time only using the second to last letter in each group. This gave her:

You are wrong

But it was the last word that caught her breath. It spelled:

Flapper

It was the stupid word her brother used.

At that moment her entire body heated up. She had done it - she cracked the code. Now she would have to rewrite the rest of the messages. Since there were so many, she knew it would take days.

And for now she didn't have time.

Valentina was on her way out the door when she heard a car pull up in front of her house. She froze, recognizing the sound of Milo's engine. She had been trying to avoid him ever since she learned he was with Larisa. So she had no interest in seeing him now.

But as Milo parked, she could tell he was determined.

About *what* she didn't know.

He got out his car and walked up to her front door.

Slowly.

When she saw his face, she opened it before he could knock, and he stood there, looking at her with those familiar brown eyes. "We need to talk."

She shook her head. "Not only am I not interested but I don't have time for this right now, Milo."

"But you always make time."

"Not today. We not friends no more, remember? You moved on and I'm moving on too."

"Why it's gotta be so different? I still love you, girl."

"Boy you love everybody! And it's not like I owe you anything, but I'm on my way to see Nevin."

Milo's expression softened. "I got it. You going to let him know."

Silence.

"Before you go anywhere, I just need a few minutes of your time."

She rolled her eyes.

"Valentina, please. You owe me after you fucked with my cousin's mind."

She knew that if she let him in, it would not end well. But she also knew that Milo was not the type of person to give up easily. And there was still the big secret she wanted to keep safe that he knew.

So, she sighed and stepped aside.

Once they were inside, Milo turned to her. "Valentina, I know I messed up. I should have never fucked with Larisa without letting you know first. But it happened so quickly."

"This is sooo tired."

"Just listen. It wasn't right and I regret it more than anything. But you can't help who you love."

"Larisa know we fucked." She grinned. "Just so you know."

"Yeah, she knew we did in the past but not the night of your party. And now she don't wanna talk to me."

"So that's what this is about?"

Valentina looked at him, her heart heavy. Hoping he would say something, anything that would make her think he wasn't trash.

"I'm asking that you tell her we good. And that you're okay with us being together. Please. Because as of now, she's cut me off."

"Milo, there are literally levels to this situation. One of them is my brother. Do you even care?"

His face fell. "I know. I just want you to know that I regret it, and I'll do anything to make it right." He moved closer and gave her the bedroom eyes. "Even do that thing you like."

She glared and shoved him back. "What, nigga? You talking about eating my pussy?"

"If you want."

"Let me make it clear...we done!" She took a deep breath. "But I do want to talk about my brother. Are you gonna give her up?"

"I'm about to eat your ass because I want to be with her. Not to give her up."

Valentina shook her head. "So this conversation is for the walls."

Milo looked at her for a moment, then nodded. "Okay, I'll leave you alone. But just know if you want to talk, ever, I'm here."

Valentina watched him walk out, her heart and mind heavy. When she heard his car pull off, she grabbed her keys and headed out the door.

CHAPTER TWENTY-ONE
TRIGGERED

DECEMBER 20th

NO RECENT MESSAGES

It was time for the truth.

And Valentina was gonna get that shit.

Sitting nervously on the edge of her brother Nevin's bed, she twisted her hands in her lap. She had rehearsed what she was going to say a hundred times, but now that the moment was there, she wasn't sure if she could go through with it.

Nevin shoved some stuff off his bed and sat across from her, his face etched with concern. "What's going on, Valentina? You look like something in your throat. Spit it the fuck out or leave."

"That's rude."

"I'm waiting."

"I cracked the text messages. And when I got one entry, the word Flapper was used."

"But you don't have the phone no more."

She glared. She hadn't told him that, so how did he know unless he broke into her shit? "Hold up, you took that phone from my house?"

"No...I...I mean...I wanted you to stop obsessing."

"You broke my fucking window, Nevin! I didn't have money for that shit."

"You got money, girl. You tell everybody that, every time you get a chance. Remember?"

"I can't believe you did that! You were so mean to me. So evil. The messages you sent took me out. And it made me think that my friends were talking about...talking about..." She couldn't believe this shit. "And yet with all that was going on, I never thought it was you. My own brother."

"Valentina, what else do you want? If it's nothing, then I need you to go."

She tried to steady her nerves. "You really don't give a fuck about me. Do you? I mean, what would make you be so foul? I gotta know."

He put on like he didn't care. "Girl, get to the point?"

She took a deep breath. "It's about your girlfriend, Nevin."

"You mean, Larisa? Your best friend." He sighed. "Because any other time you act like your relationship with her is more important than mine."

He sounded sassy. Of course she should have known the messages were from him.

"You do too much sometimes, Nevin."

He laughed. "Maybe...maybe not. But what's–."

"She cheating on your ass."

Nevin's face looked as if it went white, and he shook his head in disbelief. "What you just say?"

"You heard me."

He got up but sat back down on the bed. "No, that's not possible. Because we have an understanding where–."

"*An understanding?*"

"Yes." He paused. "She would never do that to me."

She didn't know what he meant by *understanding,* but she could tell he was in a bad mood. "Brother, I–."

"Why do you always gotta start shit? How come you can't leave things alone? Huh? What is it about you and not letting people be happy? It doesn't make any sense! Fuck!"

"Hold up, you mad at me?"

"I just told you why. You a shit starter!"

"And you a window breaker! And a phone stealer!"

"Bitch, that was my phone!" He yelled. "Just get out!"

"Okay...Okay..." Valentina reached out to take her brother's hand, but he pulled away. "Listen, I wish I could say it's not true, Nevin, but it's a fact. And the only reason I'm bringing it to you is–."

"Let me say it for you, you *love me*."

"Yes."

"Man, get the fuck out my face with all this bullshit. You not capable of loving nobody but yourself. I mean think about it, when have you ever compromised for somebody else? Huh? Never! Not once!"

"Now I know you got your feelings hurt. And I'm so sorry about that. But I'm not the enemy. As a matter of fact I should be mad at you."

"Except you are the enemy."

Valentina remained silent and looked at him closer. "Wait a minute...you not mad at me for telling you she was cheating, you're mad at me because you knew."

Silence.

"Nevin, am I lying? Did you already know she was sleeping around on you? And do you not care because of whoever you were talking to on that phone?"

He looked at her and flopped back on the bed. "It's not like that."

"Well did you know she was cheating with Milo?"

He looked down. "Milo? She's too tall for him."

"Why would you be with someone who cheats, Nevin? And what's up with that phone? Tell me something because this ain't making sense."

"It's a lot you don't know, Valentina. And I know that bothers you, but not everything is about you. I been saying it from the jump. You believe me now? Because you done burned down Pumpkin's house, got Shug locked up and Marcus raped and put in jail all because of a phone that belonged to me." He touched his chest.

Hearing the details made her shiver.

Karma would return, she was sure.

"Now Larisa is top notch. She looks good on my arm and when I take her with me to them office parties, people finally see me. And I like that shit. Because it doesn't always happen."

"You don't need a woman to–."

"Please stop!" He waved the air. "Because you don't know what you talking about."

"I do. You're my brother and you deserve more than this. And you know how I feel about that girl but still!"

"You fucking don't get it! You...you just don't get it!"

"Nevin, you can get any girl you–."

"Don't say it!"

She threw her hands up. "Okay, okay I won't. I just...I just...I will never understand this shit that's all."

"Maybe it's not for you to understand."

"You playing yourself if you stay with a woman who feels like she can cheat on you. I do know that shit. I mean y'all were supposed to get married but them little nuptials would look foolish now. Considering she–"

"You know what, for most of my life I let you say anything you wanted out your mouth. I let you do anything you wanted to our foster parents even though it would mean they would throw us out. Because you older than me. But this time you went too far. And if my world falls apart–."

"Your world already breaking. That's what you need to know." She walked up to him. "I'm gonna find out who you were texting on that phone. Believe that shit." She moved for the door.

"Valentina."

She stopped.

"Please leave it alone," tears rolled down his cheek. "I don't wanna lose you too."

"I'm sorry, Nevin. But I can't. If you won't tell me, I gotta figure it out."

CHAPTER TWENTY-TWO
ON THE RUN

Valentina sat nervously on the edge of her aunt's couch, wringing her hands together in a swirl of hate and confusion. There was a roast that was cooking in the oven which usually meant a good time was underway. But now the smell made Valentina's stomach sick.

"What is it, girl? You done drove me crazy with this silent shit."

"Auntie, I need you to tell me about my parents," Valentina said, her voice shaking.

"Okay..." Her aunt leaned forward, giving her full attention. "When you were younger you lived with your parents in Bladensburg, Maryland. And one day a tornado came, and they went up in the storm, never to be found again. Y'all were in a tow truck and–"

"Stop..." Valentina trembled softly. "I want the truth."

Jessie stared into the distance.

"The truth, auntie."

"But it is the truth. Your parents flew away in a–."

"Please, Aunt Jessie! Please!"

It was a deep long breath. "Your parents left you and your brother in an abandoned car in a liquor store parking lot. During a very violent storm. When the truck was about to haul it away, they didn't know you and your brother were inside. So the tow truck placed the car on a flatbed and lifted the vehicle up. That's when they saw your face and Nevin and his doll from the window."

"That wasn't my doll?"

"No. I don't believe it was because he kept it for four years." She sighed. "Anyway, you were six and Nevin was three."

Valentina looked down.

"After that, as you know you were taken into foster care because I couldn't afford to keep you. That weighed on me because you had a rough period, until you lived with Ms. Alexander."

"I never blamed you."

"I know. But I blamed myself." She paused. "Anyway, Ms. Alexander was old but somehow managed to take you and Nevin in, along with Pumpkin, Shug, RoRo, and Milo. To the best of her abilities she did okay. And on the weekends, I would come by and pick you all up. It was rough in the beginning. But over the years with the new clothes and money you always had, I figured the woman was a saint."

Valentina smiled. "I used to love to hear you tell me that tornado story. Because it hurt...it hurt so much to say out loud that my mother didn't want us."

"My sister and Tyrone had their reasons. Although I'll never understand a woman leaving her kids the way she did you two." She paused. "Anyway, before Ms. Alexander you made a life stealing out of people's cars, opened doors or even trash cans for food. But that woman...she really saved y'all. And I'm forever grateful."

The tears fell harder.

"Thank you for reminding me of the truth, because I...I started to forget it since the lie was so good to me. To the point where the weather...and the storm always made me feel like something I loved would be taken away."

"What is it, Valentina? You know you can tell me anything."

"If something happens to me, I need you to promise me you'll sell everything I own. The jewelry, TVs, laptop, and my vehicles. All of it. I don't have much else. When you do, give half to

Nevin and you take the rest. I already gave you power of attorney just in case."

"I don't like this." Her aunt's eyes widened in shock. "You been beating around the bush, and I allowed you to because you grown. But what kind of trouble is it where I gotta sell off your possessions like you dead?"

Valentina hesitated, not wanting to reveal too much. But she knew she couldn't keep it from her aunt any longer.

So she went into detail.

She talked more about the cell phone. And how she figured out strange cryptic messages that linked to Nevin. She went into detail about later getting messages on her personal phone, and how after a while, the original phone was stolen back by her brother.

She even mentioned how hunting for the truth put her in line with Brian and his evil.

When it was all said and done, her aunt knew enough to feel her struggle.

"Why would you hide this from me?"

"I didn't want you to get hurt."

"Don't you know if you going through something, I'll be hurt anyway? Can't you see that?"

"There's more. I did something back in the day, and I'm afraid it's going to catch up with me in addition to this strange man asking for money. It's like my entire life is falling apart. And it may be what I deserve."

"Come here, Valentina."

She walked to the sofa and sat next to her. "You will get through this. I don't know why I feel it in my heart, but I do. And when it happens you must right the wrongs that you caused. Only then will you feel free."

"But what if I lose everything?"

"You can't lose what's yours. And that's peace of mind." She touched the side of her face. "Now, can I help with anything?"

"I will call on you if I need you."

She nodded. "But listen, make it right with your brother."

"Nah, he hates me too much and I'm not too thrilled with his ass right now either."

"Call him. If something happens to you, do you want hate to be the last thing you two share?" She laughed. "Now hug me again and do what you gotta do to get your life back in order."

CHAPTER TWENTY-THREE
BIT

I t was pitch black outside.

And a storm was in play.

But she couldn't worry about entertaining her fears. She had to get the nigga's money or else.

Slowly, Valentina crept through the quiet suburban streets, her black hood pulled up over her head to conceal her face. Fully prepared, she had a navy-blue backpack slung over her shoulder, and a flashlight clutched in her palm. To keep her identity a secret, her rental car had been parked away from the scene so a camera couldn't catch the plate.

Using the information Larisa gave her, she had been snatching packages off porches for hours. With a lot of them already secured safely in her trunk, she wanted more.

A bad move.

Luckily the neighborhood she was in was like home. She knew the streets like the back of her hand, knew which houses were vacant, which neighbors were nosy, and which porches kept packages due to their owners coming home late from work.

As she approached the last house with an overhang, she paused to listen for any signs of movement inside the dwelling. It wasn't easy due to the trees rustling, but she was doing her best and for the moment was okay. Hearing nothing, she crept up to the porch and scanned the deliveries with her flashlight.

When she spotted a large box with a label that read "Fragile" she grinned. She would learn later that several laptops were inside due to the owner starting a new business.

For now they belonged to her.

Quickly she reached out to grab the box, but as her fingers closed around it, a sudden clap of thunder echoed through the neighborhood. She froze, her heart pounding in her chest. Looking up at the sky she saw it had begun to rain, the drops coming down hard and fast. She knew she had to act quickly so she turned to leave.

A door opened behind her.

Not again.

Valentina moved toward a large bush, attempting to tuck herself behind it as her heart pounded harder. The thorns of the branches stabbed at her side.

"Who's there?" A male voice called out.

Valentina didn't answer.

"I said who is in front of my fucking house?"

Silence.

When Valentina heard footsteps moving in her direction, she hit it quickly. As the wind and the water smacked against her face she ran even faster. Valentina faced close calls before but this time stealing the packages was life depending.

She needed the money.

She didn't stop until she was blocks away, the rain drenching her body as it flooded from the sky. Hiding under the ramp of a warehouse, she caught her breath before walking to her rental.

Sitting in the backseat, she opened the box and checked its contents. Yep...they were computers. Coupled with the other packages she stole; this was a good haul. But her night was long from over.

Driving back to her hideout, a small, abandoned house on the outskirts of Baltimore city, she knew she was safe there as she opened all the boxes. Looking at the product, she couldn't help but feel a sense of satisfaction.

Maybe shit finally going my way.

LATER

Valentina walked into the dimly lit warehouse, as she dragged behind her, on a cart, all her haul for the night. She had heard about this place for months, but usually Jacob did this kind of thing for her.

But he hadn't reached out.

Just gave her the information.

And so she was left alone to deal with people who were known murderers, to pay off a blackmailer she was unfamiliar with.

"Over here," a voice called out from the darkness.

She blinked a few times and spotted him sitting at a makeshift table in the corner, surrounded by a group of menacing-looking niggas with, as far as she could tell, rape on the mind.

The leader was a tall dark skinned, muscular man with a scar running down his cheek and cold, steely gray eyes that seemed to bore into her soul.

She was told his name was Andive, but she forgot it already due to fear.

Valentina approached them. "Thanks...thanks for seeing me."

They groaned as if she were annoying.

She swallowed. "I understand you're looking for electronics," she said, her eyes flicking nervously to the thugs.

Andive sneered, "*Electronics* huh?" He laughed. "You sound like police."

Her heart dropped. "I...I'm not."

"Why you here, girl?"

She was confused. "I told you."

He stepped closer, not appreciating her tone. "I'm not your fucking friend. We not equal. So be careful how you talk to me."

"I'm sorry, I just wanted to move this stuff quickly."

"Why you in a rush?"

"Because I...I need the money." She looked down. "And Jacob said you usually bought my stuff so," Valentina took a deep breath and pulled the cart closer as if it were a cute child. "I have high-quality shit here. And nothing has been used."

"I met with you because Jacob is family. Otherwise I would just take your shit and be done with it." His expression softened, and he leaned forward, studying the packages. Looking at his man he said, "Look it over."

He stepped up, grabbed the cart, and pulled it into the darkness.

Valentina, the leader, and the rest of their men stood in front of one another not saying a word.

For a moment, Valentina felt like this would be her last day alive. There was too much suspense and tension in the building for her to survive. There were so many things that could go wrong, and she prayed they wouldn't.

Fifteen minutes later, the man returned and whispered in the leader's ear.

The leader nodded and looked at her. "Okay, I'm interested. Let's talk."

Valentina breathed a sigh of relief and began to negotiate the terms of the sale. She wanted eight thousand dollars for everything, but he gave her five grand. Just enough to get Brian off her back for a little while but not enough to pay her bills in the future.

But what could she do?

Reluctantly the deal was made, and he handed her a wad of cash.

Instead of leaving she remained.

"Fuck you want now? I gave you the paper."

"Can I get my cart back? I'll be moving soon and–"

"Nah."

Valentina nodded, and quickly turned, making her way out the warehouse. With her car parked a few blocks away, she walked down the dark, narrow alley and the rain began to pour again, drenching her even more.

She was almost near her car when she heard a low growl. "You've got to be kidding me," she said before slowly looking behind her.

The growl grew deeper.

There, in the shadows, she saw a large, snarling Doberman pinscher. Its eyes were wild, and its teeth were baring.

With spread out fingers she backed slowly up and said, "Easy, doggy. Don't–"

It lunged.

Not knowing what else to do, Valentina screamed and took off running. Slipping on the pavement due to the rain, the dog's jaws closed around her arm like a bracelet, and she felt its teeth sink into her flesh. "Get off me! Get...get off!"

The animal continued to bite, whipping its head from left to right with her flesh still in its grasp.

"Help! Help! Please!"

She thought it was over, until she remembered she had something in her pocket. Reaching deep, she pulled out her spiral metal keychain spike and poked the animal in the eye. It let out a loud squeal before running down the alley and out of sight.

When she looked down at her arm she saw damage, but at least she was alive.

After parking her car, Valentina walked down the dimly lit street to meet Brian. She had heard about a dog kennel on the outskirts of town and decided that it would be the perfect place to confront him. Plus they were familiar with dog bites and patched up her arm.

Standing in the back, she saw him walk inside. A handsome but even grin on his face. He approached her. "There she goes."

"I know you've been following me for the past couple of days," she said, trying to keep her voice steady. "Even though I was getting the money."

"Yeah, I was," he replied. "Never denied it. I just wanted to make sure you knew I was serious."

Valentina reached into her pocket and pulled out the cash she earned earlier in the day. "Here," she said, holding it out to him. "It's all I got in the world."

He looked down at it and smiled. "Poor thing."

She rolled her eyes. "This is the last time," she said. "I never want to see you again. Not at my house. Not in the shadows. I don't wanna see you anywhere."

"Aww...and here I was thinking we were becoming good friends."

"I'm serious."

The smile wiped away from his face. "Are you still under the impression that you're in charge?"

"I didn't say–."

"You don't tell me what the fuck to do!" He pointed at the ground. "I tell you!"

The dogs barked louder, and she swallowed the lump in her throat. "Here...take the money. I just want this shit over with."

He yanked the cash and stuffed it into his pocket. "I hear you," he winked, his mood turned powerful. "But you know, I could make it worth your while to keep seeing me again if I wanted to."

Valentina's blood boiled with anger.

He grinned. "Besides, I like having a reason to follow you around." She watched him go, touching a few dog cages along the way.

CHAPTER TWENTY-FOUR
POUR

The rain cascaded down in sheets, drenching the pavement and illuminating the darkness with an ethereal glow. When she stepped out of her Tesla and sprinted towards the house the rain was so powerful it was almost impossible to see, but she knew the way to her door by heart.

Her hair plastered to her face and her clothes stuck to her skin as she fumbled with her keys. Just then she noticed a figure sitting on her porch holding a red umbrella. It was her ex-best friend, Larisa, clutching a plastic bag filled with Cut Water coolers.

Valentina's heart sank until she saw her pretty face, relieved it wasn't Brian.

Still, the last thing she wanted was to deal with her drama right now.

"Hey, Valentina," Larisa called out, her voice barely audible over the sound of the storm. "I'm surprised you out here like this." She looked up at the sky. "Hold up, what happened to your arm? Why is it bandaged up?"

"Leave it."

"Okay, well, I wanna talk." Larisa gave her shelter under the umbrella.

"What you wanna run your mouth about now?" Valentina asked, her voice cold and distant. "Because I'm busy."

"Did you get the packages?"

"You know I did."

Since she only received exactly $5000 from selling the stolen goods, she had to pinch off from her own money to pay Larisa her portion.

She reached into her pocket and extended her cut.

"Keep it."

She frowned. "But what about moving?"

"You sound like you need it more than me right now."

Normally Valentina would try and save face, but it was true. She did need every dime. "I hope it gets you out the bind. I really do."

She placed it back into her pocket. "Larisa, you can't buy me."

"Not trying to," she looked into her eyes. "But we been friends for a long time. And that means something to me." She paused. "Um, did you tell Nevin yet?"

"So that's what this about? You want me to keep lying to my brother?"

"Girl, no! I want our friendship back. And tonight I'll prove it. Because trust, you'll want to hear what I have to say. So can we please, just talk? In your house where it's dry?"

Valentina looked at Larisa, her eyes filled with a mix of anger and sadness. She was tired of the constant drama and back-and-forth with her ex-best friend. But she couldn't help but feel a twinge of sadness and longing for their friendship.

"Fine," Valentina said, unlocking her front door. "But if you don't make more sense out of all of this shit, we're done for good."

Larisa nodded, relief and gratitude clear on her face.

As they walked up the stairs and into Valentina's house, the storm raged on outside, and inside there was a sense of seriousness.

First, it was time to grub.

Because true to the point whenever Valentina was nervous, she prepared food. As she stood at her kitchen counter, carefully slicing up blocks of cheddar and gouda cheese, she placed the pieces on a plate, arranging them neatly next to a bowl of crackers. As she worked, she couldn't help but think about the mysterious conversation she knew was coming.

Larisa walked into the kitchen; her face etched with concern as she leaned in the doorway. "I know you solved some of the messages, have you solved the rest?"

"No...been getting money for this thing that...you know what...it doesn't matter. Are you ready to tell me what's up?"

"It's about your brother and RoRo," she said, helping her place the plate of cheese and crackers on the table.

Valentina hesitated for a moment before sitting down and reaching for a cracker. "Okay, I'm listening," she said, taking a bite.

"Your brother and RoRo fucking, girl," Larisa began, her voice shaking. "For months now."

Valentina's eyes widened in shock. "You...you playing right?"

"Nah...and I'm so sorry."

"I...this..."

Larisa remained silent and took a seat across from her at the table. "It's true, girl."

Valentina shook her head, tears welling up in her eyes. "I don't...I don't understand why you would say some shit like that. I need you...I need you to tell me more."

Larisa looked down. "Years ago Nevin got drunk and told me who he was at the house when you and Milo were fucking in your room. I was trying to give him some pussy, but he pushed me back." She sighed remembering the embarrassment. "Anyway, he was afraid to come out as gay, especially when he learned his boss was homophobic. Which is crazy because why are you homophobic when you own male clothing stores?"

"It's like everybody around me got a secret life." Valentina said.

"One day the man straight up made a gay joke in front of everybody at one of their stores. It was an assumption and Nevin hated that shit. I did too. So we came up with a plan for me to be his fake girlfriend." She shook her head. "You should have seen us when we went to his work Christmas party as a couple. His boss was stuck and Nevin was so happy about the compliments we got. The next day he said he would pay me if I told everybody we were getting married. I said yes. I needed the money to move. And we called it an *understanding*."

"But...how long has he been this way?"

"From what he told me, since he was little. He blamed himself for y'all not having a home due to your father saying he was too soft, and I felt him on that shit, Valentina."

"But he always had girlfriends."

"Yeah, masculine women who ended up leaving him for other women." She shook her head. "When I stayed at his house, that's one of the things we talked about. How lonely it must've been not to have anybody."

"But how could you put yourself out for a gay man?"

"At the time I was single and didn't care but now...with Milo...things are different."

"I wish you would've...would've said something."

"I couldn't do it to Nevin."

"I knew your relationship came out of nowhere." Valentina wiped her hair behind her ear. "I never even seen y'all hug except for that one time he kissed you on the neck at my party."

"He was doing too much that night." Larisa took a deep breath. "I think he was drunk."

Valentina stood up and backed into the refrigerator.

"You want me to go on?"

234

Valentina nodded slowly.

"Well, I didn't know about RoRo until a few days ago. Milo mentioned he saw them at the movies a little too close. So I'm bringing it to you. So you know it's not just me and Milo. Nevin is at fault too."

"My brother is actually gay?" She whispered.

Larisa nodded.

"Why didn't he...why didn't he feel like he could tell me this?"

"You know why."

Tears welled up in her eyes. "I don't. I'm for real."

"You're too judgmental." Larisa stood up and reached out to take Valentina's hand. "And that shit be hurting when niggas ain't in the mood. People are going through serious things, girl. And a joke ain't always funny."

"Now I get why he came at me so hard on them text messages. He wanted me to feel pain. Like he did."

"Wait, the messages were from him?"

"Yeah."

"Wow. I'm so sorry. I can't even imagine how you must be feeling right now. I just wanted you to know the truth."

Valentina sniffled, wiping away her tears. "I don't know what to do. It's like everything I knew was a lie."

Larisa squeezed her hand again. "You can be mad, but after that you need to talk to your brother."

Valentina nodded, taking a deep breath although she was nowhere near letting it go. "I need some time to process everything."

"Of course." Larisa hugged her tightly. "If you have time, and you don't believe me, solve the rest of the texts and you'll see what I'm saying is true." She released her.

"Nah...I'm off that shit."

"I don't blame you," she giggled. "Anyway, when you ready, hopefully we can get back to us. Because I don't know how you feel, but I miss you like shit."

Truth finally came into her life.

And Valentina wasn't sure if she could handle it.

CHAPTER TWENTY-FIVE
NEXT LIFE

Valentina groggily opened her eyes to the smell of bacon and eggs wafting through the air as she slept in her bedroom. Pushing the large pillows away that momentarily covered her face, she sat up in bed, rubbing her eyes and trying to shake off the remnants of sleep.

As she woke up even more, she could hear pots and pans clanging in the kitchen, signaling that someone was cooking breakfast. "Please don't let that man be in my house," she said, speaking of Brian.

After slipping on her one-piece red nightgown and grabbing her spiral key chain weapon still tinged with dog blood, she made her way to the kitchen. Slowly she bent the corner.

Who was in her fucking house?

Although seconds passed, it felt like hours when the kitchen came into view. She breathed a sigh of relief when she saw her brother, Nevin, standing at the stove, flipping pancakes.

With a hand on her chest she said, "Boy, you scared the fuck out of me." She dropped the keys on the counter. "Used your key huh? Couldn't you have done that instead of breaking my window?"

"You would've known it was me." He shook his head and giggled. "You avoid cameras so much you didn't even bother to put one on your home."

"I'm not laughing. Larisa told me everything. About you being–"

"Stop." He looked over. "I know. So first let's start by saying I'm here to make you breakfast, before I give my part of the story."

Valentina frowned, still a bit confused.

Walking deeper into the kitchen she grabbed the seat, pulled it out and flopped down at the table. "I thought you didn't want to see me anymore."

Nevin shook his head. "Like I said, I just wanted to surprise you with breakfast and then talk. Nothing more, nothing less." He squinted. "What's wrong with your arm?"

"I got bit."

She wanted to talk about what she learned from Larisa. She didn't know if she was mad that someone else told her or that he obviously didn't trust her enough to let her know.

"Are you okay? I could–."

"Shouldn't you have called? Especially after you pretty much told me to get fucking lost. And then my window...you broke it. No apology. No offer to pay for it. Just nothing. I mean, if you wanted your cell phone, why not ask for it back instead of torturing me?"

"I was embarrassed. Still am now." With the spatula still in hand he said, "And I was...I was wrong. So I wanted to come over here to tell you that and apologize in my own way. And trust me it is sooo hard to do."

"What about the red hat?"

He sighed. "Larisa told me about it, and Marcus, so I put it on your lawn."

"If you knew the things I had Jacob do to him. This is so fucked up!" She shook her head. "I haven't even been getting sleep. I'm stressed all the time."

"I'm sorry. But I thought you would be fine since you on them pills."

"I haven't used them in days." She had so many questions and they were pouring out of her. "Who was the text message to? The one that said, *'I'm gonna fuck up her life. Trust.'*?"

"Oh...RoRo had been ignoring me. And you, of all people knows he fucked with females back in

239

the day so...so I thought he was fucking a co-worker. It ended up being some nigga at work messing his life up. I'm sorry. This...this was wrong on so many levels. I was trying to throw you off so you could leave it alone and not investigate the phone, but you wouldn't let it go." He shook his head. "I truly am embarrassed."

She knew that Nevin had always been there for her. The way she treated him sometimes was probably the reason he lied about his lifestyle. But this was vicious.

They sat down at the kitchen table and started to eat a spread of bacon, cheese eggs, pancakes, and spiked coffee with cream. When the meal was almost done, he began talking about his life.

As they chatted, Valentina noticed that Nevin seemed a bit on edge. He kept fidgeting with his fork and avoiding her gaze. "You probably don't remember, but when I was little our father...I mean."

"Nevin, it's okay." She touched his hand. "For real."

"He thought I was gay because I liked...I liked dolls." He sighed. "I was very young, but I remember that this nigga was soooo fucking mean to me. So hateful. And I kept that shit on my heart even when I probably didn't need to." He breathed deeply. "Me liking dolls, and being the way I was, was the reason they left." He looked down. "The reason they abandoned us. And I didn't want you to abandon me too if you found out."

"I would never do that shit!"

"That's what I felt!"

"Nevin, I was mean to you. But that's little brother and sister shit. I love you. Would die for you!"

"It doesn't feel that way."

"I know and I'm sorry. But you are not the reason they left." She said, looking over at him. "What happened to us is not our fault. It's not your fault. Our family left because...because they were bad parents. That's fucking it!" She paused. "Wait right here." She ran out of the room and returned with the book. "These are the messages. I haven't decoded the rest and I don't want to."

His body melted in the chair, and he appeared to be on the verge of a breakdown. Like he couldn't breathe as he looked down at it.

"Are you okay, Nevin?"

"Uh...yeah." He flipped it open. "These messages remind me of how sad we were and..."

"You sure you okay?"

"Uh...actually..." He touched his head.

"Nevin, you're scaring me."

Nevin stood up abruptly. "Sorry, sis, I gotta use the bathroom," he mumbled, and quickly ran off.

Valentina sat there for a moment, dumbfounded.

Did she say too much? Did she not say enough? She couldn't shake the feeling that despite everything he learned that he was still holding back. And she wasn't about to play the games anymore.

It was time to get sneaky to see what her little brother was going through.

She decided to peek at Nevin's phone which he left on the table.

Before grabbing it, she looked to make sure he wasn't coming. She would use the sound of water and the toilet flushing to let her know she didn't have any more time.

With the iPhone in her hand, she entered his birthday plus her birthday. She knew his code because he had given it to her many times to take pictures and send messages. Her knowing the code was probably another reason he had a burner.

After the cell was opened, she scrolled through his texts. With some fast quick reading, she saw something devastating. A conversation so final it made her heart feel as if it had stopped.

The toilet flushed.

The water ran.

Suddenly, Nevin returned.

He stopped in his tracks when he saw Valentina with his phone in her hand. She meant to put it down. Had plans to put it down, but what she saw on it broke her heart.

"Why do you have my shit, Valentina?"

"Nevin, what are you and RoRo about to do?"

"Valentina, I can explain," he said with a worried tone.

She looked at him, her eyes wide with shock. "What's going on, Nev? Are you...are you planning to take your life?"

Nevin took a deep breath, walked over to her, grabbed her hand, and told her everything.

"RoRo stole money from that tax service company he works for. The thing is the dude that knows is now saying he's gonna tell if we don't give him $50,000 even though he already been giving him money."

Valentina sat back in the chair. "Nevin..."

"And he can't make it in prison." He cried. "And I can't lose him. Not when I finally found love. And finally found me." She could see the pain and guilt etched on his face, and she knew that he had been struggling with this for a long time.

"I'm sorry, Valentina," he said. "I should have told you sooner. I hope you can forgive–."

"He's blackmailing me now." She placed the phone on the table. "This...this bitch is now blackmailing me after he did this shit to RoRo!"

"Wait...that's the person you were talking about?"

"It sounds like it."

She went on to tell him how she followed RoRo when she found the cell phone and was worried he was working with police. And how the man had been threatening her ever since. She told him every single thing and Nevin was furious.

"We aren't supposed to talk about that night," Nevin said with wide eyes. "I mean you, me and the others."

"I know. But when all of this went down, I was scared. Thinking that the pact was broken." She paused. "I mean, didn't you want me to think that when you sent the texts?"

His eyes widened. "Oh my, God! I was talking about porch pirating! Not the other thing." He put his hand over his chest. "No wonder you were going crazy!"

Slight relief washed over her.

"Anyway, I know you're scared, Nevin," she said softly. "Everything that has been happening to us is my fault. And I'm gonna make it right. Just…just give me some time. I promise, I'm gonna get that money."

CHAPTER TWENTY-SIX
REGRETS

Valentina sat alone in her dimly lit room, staring at her phone.

Her brother needed help, which meant she had to do the right thing for once in her life. First, she needed to sell all her shit. But because her ultimate plan could mean she may get hurt, she needed to admit to something.

She needed to give a confession.

With a deep breath, she pressed the record button on her phone and began to speak.

"Hey, it's Valentina Cash and I want to come clean about something. Something that has been bothering me for a long time."

MANY YEARS AGO

The room was silent except for the sound of snow hitting the windows. Six adults huddled together in their childhood bunkbed room, whispering words barely audible to one another.

Before this moment, when Valentina was 16, Nevin was 13, Rowan was 14, Milo was 17, and Pumpkin and Shug were 15, they all stole money from Ms. Alexander, their elderly foster mother.

But when they became adults, they took the crime further, by buying cars, opening utility accounts, and even using credit cards in her name. Mainly because they all kept in contact with her over the years.

Later, when Ms. Alexander discovered it, she summoned them all to the home they grew up in as kids. Letting them know that if they didn't tell the truth, she would go to the police and explain how all of them were involved, as they also wiped her savings accounts clean.

They were federally fucked if she ever said a word.

Valentina was ill that day, as she had been suffering from an infection that at the time, she wasn't aware of so this was the worst day of her life. "This is all your fault, Valentina," Shug said, her voice quivering. "You came up with this shit not us."

"But I did it for us. I did it because she had been letting her kids take our money while we lived like

247

we were homeless," Valentina whispered. "I mean think about how we all lived. Boys and girls in this same room. Dirty clothing at school. She didn't even bother to hide it while she lived like a queen. I mean it wasn't right."

"Exactly, but you're the one who suggested it," Milo pointed out. "And now we're all in this mess."

"What if we just tell the truth," Pumpkin said softly, her eyes downcast. "Tell them how Ms. Alexander mistreated us. Then we take the blame and face the consequences."

"You sound crazy," Milo said.

"All I'm saying is, I don't think Valentina should deal with this shit alone. She's right...at one point stealing the money was about food when we were young. But afterward every last one of us kept pressing the issue for more, even when Valentina said no." She looked at Shug. "I mean ain't your apartment in Ms. Alexander's name?"

Shug sighed. "So you want us all to go to prison? For the rest of our lives?"

The room fell silent, each of them lost in their own thoughts.

Suddenly, the sound of Ms. Alexander's rocking chair creaking in the living room wafted through the air. Her dog, a Doberman pinscher, growled every so often at the door. He didn't trust naire one of them niggas.

"She's waiting for us," Nevin said, his voice barely above a whisper. "We need to decide what to do."

"Please help us, Valentina," Shug cried. "We not strong like you. We don't have a YouTube channel or whatever. All of us still in the streets. Please...I can't be in jail."

"Shouldn't that be the reason you go to jail?" Nevin said. "Since your life ain't about shit?"

"Fuck you," Shug said.

"I don't want my sister locked up," Nevin said. "So whatever we do, that can't be the plan."

"I don't want her locked up either!" Pumpkin responded.

Rowan remained silent, too afraid to say a word.

As they spoke amongst themselves Shug said, "We could always call Jacob."

The room went hush, all knowing what her boyfriend was capable of. Born to parents who had been on prescription drugs all their lives, he didn't have an emotional connection to anyone but Valentina.

"Are you sure?" Valentina asked. "Because if I do it, I need a yes from each one of you."

The room got quieter before...

"Yes..." from Milo.

"Yeah." From Pumpkin.

In the end, everyone said yes.

Valentina nodded, pulled out her cell phone and dialed Jacob's number. "Where are you?"

"At our apartment. Where you at? You still feel bad?"

"Jacob, the thing Ms. Alexander wanted to talk to us about is not looking good. And I need you to do what you do," she said, her voice trembling.

"Fuck would you ask me something like that for? And over the phone at that."

She gave him the details, or more like lies. She said her kids had stolen money and were trying to put it on the foster children. And that if things continued, she would be locked up for a crime she didn't commit. And the last thing that man wanted to do was lose her.

She was all he had.

"You know I don't fuck with old people and babies." He paused. "Only niggas who got it coming. And you really asking me to do this shit?" He asked angrily.

"I have no choice, baby. Please."

The others listened in stunned silence, as Jacob's voice came through the phone. "If we do this, things will never be the same between us."

She didn't believe him. "I need you. Do what you do."

"I'm on my way."

"What are y'all gonna do in there?" Ms. Alexander called out. "Because in fifteen minutes I'm calling the police!"

"We still talking," Milo yelled.

Twenty minutes later, they heard Ms. Alexander opening the door, followed by the sound of Jacob's footsteps. The dog barked a few times and then went silent. He had been given some laced meat by Jacob and was out cold.

"What's going on, Jacob? You here to pick up Valentina?" Ms. Alexander asked, having been familiar with him since he was young. "And what you just give Rex?"

Silence.

They remained huddled in the room, when suddenly, the sound of Ms. Alexander and Jacob's voices grew loud. There was a thud, followed by rattling, before things went deathly quiet.

It was done.

When the front door closed, they remained in that old room, waiting.

It was Valentina who moved first. It was Valentina who opened the door and it was Valentina who found Ms. Alexander in her rocking chair, unresponsive.

She had been suffocated.

A hand to the nose and mouth.

Then they set the place on fire, burning everything in sight. And since Ms. Alexander was a chain smoker, they started the blaze near her body with her own cigarettes to cover up the murder.

But every person in the room knew the deal. Most tried to forget. Hell, even Valentina put it behind her until she found the cell phone in her bathroom.

Guilt had a way of scratching up the past.

Valentina lost a lot that night. First it was her peace of mind. Then it was her ability to trust. But later it was Jacob who bounced when she was admitted to the hospital due to an infection that ravished her body.

Valentina's life had never been the same.

After making the confession on a recording, which exonerated everyone but herself, she breathed deeply, grabbed the Hennessy bottle, and took a fat ass gulp.

Next, she went over her plan to help Nevin.

She would sell most of her things to raise enough money, in the hopes that if her plan A didn't work, Brian would leave her people the fuck alone. When that was over, she made a list of everything of value. When she was done, she drank half the bottle of Hennessy, and made the hardest call ever.

Within minutes a deal was made.

It was a sunny afternoon when she saw the red and yellow tow truck float down the street. Walking outside as if she were going to her own funeral she watched as the truck came to a stop in front of her home and focused on the sound of its engine dying down.

With the bottle of liquor in hand, she stared at a middle-aged man with a mustache who parked haphazardly, one wheel on the curb. He stepped out, slamming the door shut before walking towards the house, his boots crunching on the gravel driveway.

"Hey," she said, taking a swig.

"The Tesla, right?" He looked to the curb.

She nodded. "Y...yeah."

He scratched his side, bobbled to the truck, grabbed his toolbox, and got to work. The sounds of his tools clanging against the pavement echoing in the quiet neighborhood as he hooked up her car was eerie because it was the same color tow truck where she and Nevin were found inside of.

Still, Valentina watched as he worked. The smell of oil and gasoline mixed with the fresh, clean scent of the neighborhood. Her feelings hurt seeing the lifestyle she built crash down but what could she do?

When the car was safely secured, the tow truck driver climbed back into the cab. With a final honk of the horn, the vehicle drove off, leaving her stuck.

Now it was time to sell her gear.

And she had a lot of it.

Expensive Louis Vuitton bags, Fendi jumpsuits, YSL garments and more.

That didn't even include her shoes and the rest of her purses. But all that shit got packed up.

Everything, leaving her sweatpants, t-shirts, and a few sneakers.

When she was done, she clutched a bag full of all her designer garments. Tears rolled down her cheek as she thought again about the lifestyle she was giving up and the memories she had associated with these possessions.

But her brother's situation had spiraled out of control, and she had to step up. She had to do whatever it took to help him, even if it meant sacrificing her own luxuries.

The next day it was garage sale time which she already advertised for. The event was scheduled for 10:00 am but they crowded the lawn at 9:15 when they saw what would be for sale. Not feeling like drawing out the inevitable, slowly she walked outside toward a group of people who were gathered around a table with her sign that read "Real Designer Clothing Sale". They were ready to increase their "worth" by taking hers.

And she knew the feeling.

"Are you selling the purses or nah?" A white woman with red hair yelled.

"You see me coming right?"

"Well hurry the hell up."

"Nah, bitch, get the fuck up out of here." Waving her hand.

She rolled her eyes, stomped feet, and drove away.

"Anybody else wanna do the most?"

They moaned and remained silent.

"That's what the fuck I thought."

Valentina rolled her eyes, took a deep breath, and started pulling her clothes out of the bag, one by one she placed them on the table. She folded each item carefully, wanting the things presented in the best light as possible for the last time. The purses stacked one behind the other but in the way the labels could be seen.

She hated seeing them paw at her items despite knowing that in a little while, they would no longer be hers.

And then she stepped back a tad but close enough to get her money.

A big woman with a sharp eye for fashion picked up a dark blue Gucci blouse and held it up to the light, studying it closely. "Is this real? It's for my daughter."

"What you think?"

"Hmmm, hmmm."

Valentina sighed deeply.

"Anyway, this is a beautiful piece," she said, looking up at Valentina. "How much you asking for it?"

"Whatever you're willing to pay," Valentina replied, trying to keep her voice steady. "As long as it's not under $100.00."

"Sold!" She yelled.

The woman handed her a pile of cash after she collected a few other items. Growing richer, Valentina felt a pang of sadness as she pocketed the money. She repeated this process with her other clothing, until everything on the table was gone.

Later that evening, she made her way over to a group of men who were inspecting a set of her high-end appliances. Their trucks dressed her curb over the hours while pickup trucks littered her lawn. She sold her refrigerator, dishwasher, and oven. The men haggled over the prices, but in the end, Valentina was able to get enough to prevent her from falling into serious depression about giving her shit away too cheaply.

As she walked away from the group and looked at the stuffed money in her raspberry-colored fanny pack, she suddenly felt a weight lift off her shoulders. She had done what she had to do to help her brother, and even though it was difficult, it was done.

The right thing ain't always the easy thing.

But it was starting to feel good.

An hour later she called her brother. "Sis...what's up?"

"Nevin, I got the money." She said into her cell phone excitedly.

"Wait...what?"

"I got the paper to pay him off. I'll give you the cash if need be, but I want to try one thing first. All I'm asking is that you and RoRo wait on me. Don't do anything that's final. I love you."

"Valentina, I...I can't accept that. This is too much. I...how did you...how? You said you were cash pour!"

"I was."

"Well I don't want you to–."

"I wanna do it." She breathed deeply. "Trust me."

"Can I do anything for you?"

"For starters I need RoRo. I need you to tell him to call me now."

"Say no more."

Valentina sat nervously at the kitchen table, sipping a glass of red wine. She had invited Jacob over and her heart fluttered when he came. Dressed in a leather jacket and with a smirk on his face, he hung in the doorway.

"Where all your shit?"

"The only thing I care about is you."

He looked down and then to the right. "What is all this about, girl?"

"I think I know what you want to hear." She played with her own fingers. "After all this time."

"I'm listening."

"I lied to you. I made you compromise yourself for me by...by hurting Ms. Alexander and I see you been hating yourself ever since." Big tears rolled. "But that's on me, baby. I know you feel like it's you but it's not. And I'm...I'm so fucking sorry."

Jacob walked in and sat in the chair, rubbing his chin. "I knew you had your shit about you but stealing from that woman when she did what she did to pull all y'all off the street was foul. And then you...and then you fucking lied to me!" A heavy fist rang out on the table.

"You're so right." She wiped her eyes. "Ms. Alexander had her shit, but she didn't deserve that and neither did you." She paused. "I took...I took advantage because I knew I was all you had. And you showed me that you were all that mattered to me when you left." She shook her head. "Because I have never been more destroyed. The only thing I want is you. And I know...I know I don't deserve you but...I gotta try."

He looked away from her pretty face. "Y'all burned her fucking house down." The words exited his lips for the first time. "Her people couldn't even give her a funeral."

"I know...and if something happens to me, I made sure none of y'all are gonna fall for that shit. I left a confession that–."

"A confession for what?" He glared.

"So you wouldn't be held responsible for–."

"The damage is done, Valentina!" He waved the air. "I don't want you locked the fuck up. Why you think I'm still around? Doing for you. Checking on you. Killing for you."

"I thought you didn't...I...want me."

"I love you, girl. But this devil...this evil in you not it. How we gonna find heaven if we both on demon time?"

She looked down.

"I just wanted...I just wanted this shit right here." He paused. "To hear the words and you gave them to me."

"Who told you?" She sniffled, so relieved. "That I lied to you about Ms. Alexander?"

"You did, when I left, and you didn't come find me until you needed something. I knew then something else was up."

"Baby...I'm...I'm sorry."

Jacob stood up and walked over to the window, staring out at the falling snow. He was silent for a moment before turning back to Valentina while leaning on the sink. "Get over here."

She couldn't believe it.

"You mean...come to you?"

"You gonna make me beg?"

Slowly she walked over to him. When their bodies connected, he wrapped his arms around her lower waist and kissed her passionately.

They had been fucking from the gate, but this felt more personal.

More loving.

Real.

Lifting her up, he maintained the weight of her body with one hand, before snaking his thickness into her center with the other. Her head fell back in joy as he handled her body as if it were a steering wheel.

He didn't have to say he loved her again.

But she could feel in that moment what was real.

And in her mind, nothing else mattered.

CHAPTER TWENTY-SEVEN
PAID IN FULL

Valentina stood outside the decrepit warehouse, her heart pounding in her chest. She clutched the bag of cash tightly in her hand, her knuckles white from the tension as she waited on the man of the hour.

Brian *The Stalking Blackmailer.*

Earlier that day she came to a settlement with him. A price she felt would be enough for him to leave RoRo alone. And she knew the details because RoRo gave them to her.

Brian accepted.

She took a deep breath, opened the large door, and made her way inside. Her footsteps echoing in the empty space. It was plenty nasty. The warehouse was dimly lit and smelled of mold and mildew and as she moved, she could hear water dripping somewhere in the distance.

Walking deeper in, she saw him sitting at a makeshift table in the center of the room. He was shrouded in shadows, but she could see the glint of the handle of a gun sitting on the table.

She almost turned around.

"I thought you didn't want to see me anymore." His tone was accusatory. "Miss me already huh?"

"I didn't. Until I found out what you were doing to my brother. And his friend."

"I thought I told you to keep our thang a secret." He paused. "I see you can't do that. But it doesn't matter. Them niggas broke anyway."

Silence.

"How I know this not a set up?" He leaned back, his arms folded over his chest.

"Because I wouldn't–."

"You wouldn't what? Lie for your brother. Or his lover."

She moved closer. "I had no business thinking I was smarter than you because I'm not. I just want this to go away."

He smiled. "Yeah, it was a dumb move. Just like RoRo."

"Can you tell me how you did it? Like, how you was able to arrange the money to be stolen? Based on what RoRo said, you found a serious glitch in their accounting system."

Suddenly he got up and said, "Bitch, you think I'm stupid? You trying to trap me? Take off your fucking clothes."

"Wha...what?"

"I said take off your fucking clothes! All of them! NOW!"

She did as she was told until she stood before him wearing only panties and a bra.

"I said everything, bitch."

Her body stood bare before his eyes.

Relieved, slowly he sat down, "You just as fine as I thought."

"Can I get dressed?" She glared.

He nodded. "I guess."

She got dressed quicker than she ever had in her life.

When she was decent, she said, "I was asking because I really wanted to know. I mean, maybe it's something I can do because as you know, I'm not living the best life."

He smiled cockily. "Well don't waste your time. I found the glitch because I built the system. And I made sure no matter what update happened, that I could always be able to siphon the money. So I did that, and I loved it."

"Thank you for telling me the–."

"But it wasn't just me. I told RoRo about it, and he started taking paper too. Then the nigga got greedy and had me taken out of accounting. So I told him I would go away if I was given a fee."

"Well how much fucking money do you need? Even if he couldn't get you no more, you should've been good with what he already gave you."

"Well I'm not and I wasn't." He paused. "RoRo ain't innocent. Before he was taken out of accounting himself, he was my boss, and he was an asshole. Made me come in all hours of the day, even when I was off the schedule. So he had all this shit coming." He took a deep breath. "Now do you have the money or not?"

Valentina nodded, her throat tight with fear. She held out the bag of cash, her hand shaking. Suspicious, he stood up, snatched the bag from Valentina's hand and looked through it thoroughly, bypassing the money.

"What you doing?" She asked.

"I should've checked it first," he said. "For a recorder."

"I told you I'm not recording you. I just want this shit over." He eyed her once more and began counting the money. "It's all there," Valentina said, her voice barely above a whisper. "All $20,000. You can have it if you leave my brother and RoRo alone."

"I asked for more from RoRo, $50,000 to be exact. Why should I take this $20,000 instead again?" He said, staring intensely. "I need reminding."

"Because some money is better than nothing."

The man nodded, his expression unreadable. "I hear you."

"It's no I hear you. I need to know we're good."

He laughed. "What did I tell you about trying to control the situation?" He leaned closer. "Don't."

Valentina watched as Brian stuffed the bag of cash into a duffel bag and slung it over his shoulder. He didn't say another word as he walked past her, his footsteps echoing out of the empty warehouse.

Once he was gone, Valentina let out a sigh of relief.

Next, she walked over to Jacob who was tucked behind some large metal structures that were there for construction. With some of the money she gained from selling her things, she had to give Jacob twenty grand to stay overnight.

Now the job was done.

She walked over to him and whispered, "Did you get the footage?"

He pulled out the camera and waved it in the air. "Yep. And I almost killed that nigga for stepping to you too." He handed her the tape. "What you gonna do now?"

"Edit out the part where he mentioned RoRo. And stop on the part where he says he's to blame." She took a deep breath. "Now with the twenty grand I have for you at home, coupled with the twenty grand you snatch back from him, you should be good. But you gotta hurry up and chase him."

He shook his head. "Nah, I know where he lives. I'ma get the bag." He looked at her closely. "But keep the other twenty stacks. Use it to get back on your feet."

She wanted to cry. "For real?"

"Helping other niggas...I like this for you," He winked and walked away.

A meeting had been called at Borders & Don Accounting Services.

The office was tense as the employees gathered around the conference table; their eyes fixed on the man at the head of the room. Brian was also there, and he was as confused as everyone else about what was going on. It was clear that something big was about to happen, and they wanted to know what the fuck they had to do with it all.

When everyone arrived, finally, the boss, Mr. Don spoke up, his voice heavy with anger. "I have some very serious news to share with all of you. It has been brought to my attention..." he cleared his throat. "That...that one of our colleagues has been engaging in reprehensible behavior." He pointed down at the table. "And this is the kind of thing I will not stand for in my company."

The employees exchanged worried glances.

"I'm talking about embezzlement. One of our own has been using information to extort money for himself. The shit stops today!"

Brian farted.

The room was silent afterwards, as Mr. Don glared at one person, who sat at the table with his head down, looking like a bitch.

"You know what I mean don't you Larry," the boss spat, pointing at him with a finger. His real name wasn't even Brian. "How could you have done this?"

Slowly his head rose. "A meeting? You do this in a meeting?"

"Yes. Because the stranger who gave this to me said you like to set people up. And I won't be caught dead in a room alone with you." He paused. "Now get out and don't ever come back. YOU'RE FIRED!"

Slowly Larry rose. "You'll be hearing from my lawyer."

"Good, because then I'll play them this." He started the recording of him speaking in detail about stealing money. "It's a good thing you got a lawyer because you will need one. We will be pressing charges. Fully. NOW GET THE FUCK OUT!"

CHAPTER TWENTY-EIGHT
CELEBRATE
MONTHS LATER

The party was in full swing at Valentina's house.

The air was thick with the scent of sweet incense coupled with the bass of the music vibrating through her chest. The walls were adorned with neon lights in a spectrum of colors, casting an otherworldly glow over the guests who were in celebration mode.

People were packed into every corner of the living room, dancing wildly to hip-hop. Some were sprawled out on metal chairs, laughing, and chatting, while others had retreated to dimly lit corners for a little privacy.

Valentina's house may have been empty, due to selling most of her items, but the atmosphere was electric as everyone caught up in the energy of the night.

After getting Larry, aka Brian, hemmed up at work, he disappeared. For a while RoRo and Nevin went into hiding too, but since it was clear Larry was gone far away due to not wanting to get locked up, they let their hair down.

Just a little.

So Valentina, always a party animal, wanted a celebration for them both.

When Valentina saw Milo and Larisa across the room, she pushed her way to the front and was met with a sea of bodies, all moving to the beat in perfect synchronization.

The vibe was contagious and sexy. Just the way she liked it.

"Y'all having fun?" She asked them.

"This is nice." Larisa grinned. "I mean I know you leaving this house, but you made things so pretty for Nevin." She looked around. "I mean look at this fucking place."

"And RoRo," she corrected her. "This is for RoRo too."

"I'm proud of you," Milo said, touching her hand. "I mean I don't know what this is all about, and I'm glad I don't but, you big for letting this lifestyle go."

She smiled. "Thank you." With a tight rock fist she hit him in the arm. "And you better be good to my friend."

Milo looked up at Larisa and kissed her lips. Then he focused on Valentina. "I'll treat her right. I'm in it for the long haul. Plus–"

Suddenly, Valentina felt a tap on her shoulder, she turned around and saw her brother Nevin. He was smiling like she hadn't seen him grin in ages.

"Valentina, this is...it's beautiful. I love you for this...for everything."

She hugged him and grabbed him by the hand, leading him away from Milo and Larisa. "I'm sorry about RoRo's job. I didn't know they would let him go but–."

He grabbed her face with both hands. "Nah, you saved him. You saved us! And he left the job he wasn't fired."

"Ohhhh..."

"And since he did it on his own accord, they can't pin anything on him in the future. I didn't think there was a way out for us and...Valentina..." He hugged her mid-sentence. "I can't tell you how grateful I am. I know it cost you everything, and I'm sorry."

"You're happy. That's all that matters."

She looked over his shoulder. "Where's RoRo anyway?"

"He's on the way. Had to make a stop to get some ice since you don't have a fridge." He inhaled. "I still can't believe you sold all your shit." He shook his head. "So where you going?"

"Already got an apartment. In my new price range."

He nodded. "How much per month?"

"Twelve hundred. I started helping other influencers get their numbers up. I got a few clients and enough rent for a year. I'll be alright."

"That's...that's not your style but–."

"It's my style now. Trust me."

He hugged her again.

She could tell he felt guilty, and she didn't want him to. "I'll be fine, Nevin. I'm happy that I'm done with all this shit and that you're safe. That's all I want."

He nodded and tears fell. "Let me go grab something to drink."

She watched as her brother made his way back into the crowd, a smile on his face. She was still grinning when suddenly the sound of wood fracturing startled everyone. Instinctively someone turned off the music as they tried to find the source of the sound through the crowd.

Valentina turned to see a figure standing in the doorway, a black ski mask covering his face and a gun in hand. He could try all he wanted to hide his identity, but Valentina knew exactly who he was.

Larry aka Brian The Blackmailer.

Nevin, who had been mingling with guests, froze in fear as the figure stepped deeper into the room. "Looks like the party's over," Larry said, his voice muffled by the mask.

"What is this about?" Valentina asked, stepping in front of her brother.

"You know what this is about, bitch! You set me up. What did you think I would do? Let it go?"

Nevin's heart raced as he realized what was happening. This was the man who was ruining their lives. He had been expecting this day to come, but he had never thought it would be like this.

"Please...please don't hurt my brother." She stepped closer. "I'm the one who got you fired. Not him."

"You should've left things alone! Now you won't forget this day for the rest of your–."

Nevin knocked her safely out of the way with all his might. When she hit the floor, he tried to make a run for the door, but Larry was too quick. And so, with a cold, calculated move, he pulled the trigger.

The first bullet ripped through Nevin's left shoulder, knocking him off balance. The next bullet hit the small of his back causing him to fall to the ground. The third and final bullet pierced his skull.

Just like that, her only brother was dead.

Valentina got to her feet, but her knees buckled under her body at the sight of her brother on the floor. "Noooooo....noooo!"

Hysteria reigned supreme in her home!

The guests screamed and ran for cover as Larry moved through the room, the gun still in hand. "Everyone, get down on the ground," he demanded, his voice cold and menacing. "I'm not fucking playing!" As everyone did as they were told, he moved even closer to Nevin's lifeless body and bent down to inspect it. "Y'all should have paid my price, Nevin. But I'll take your life instead."

With that, he turned and ran out, leaving behind a trail of terror and death.

Valentina fainted.

CHAPTER TWENTY-NINE
NEW LIFE

Thes sky was a dull gray, the clouds thick and heavy with the promise of rain.

The air was weighed with humidity, making it hard to breathe physically and emotionally. The streets were slick with a light mist that clung to everything it touched causing things outside of the vehicle to blur.

The only sound was the steady hum of the car's engine as Valentina, Larisa, and Milo drove away from Nevin's funeral, each lost in their own thoughts. The overcast weather seemed to mirror their somber moods, as they grappled with the weight of their loss and the uncertainty of what the future held.

Larry had been arrested and charged with embezzlement and murder. But why didn't it make anybody feel better?

The shit still hurt.

Deeply.

Valentina sat in the back seat of the car, staring out the window as Larisa drove. Milo sat in the passenger seat, his head in his hands. The silence was suffocating.

"I can't believe this shit," Milo whispered to no one in particular.

"Me either," Larisa muttered. "I mean...did you see RoRo? Did you see him throw his body on the–."

"Stop, baby," Milo said, having seen the casket rock when he cried as he gripped it.

It was a sad day.

Valentina's brother, Nevin Cash, had been taken from them too soon, and the pain of losing him was still raw like freshly butchered meat.

"What am I gonna do without my brother?" She whispered, her forehead dropping on the cool window.

Larisa looked back but remained silent. Besides, what else could she say? She didn't have the answers.

No one did for that matter.

"I feel like it's a nightmare that I can't wake up from. Can somebody help me?" She cried harder. "Please, somebody help me."

Milo looked up, his eyes red and puffy. "I can't believe that mothafucka came in and just took a member of our family like he was nothing."

"I'm just grateful that they got his ass!" Larisa said. "He better get the death penalty for this shit."

"Naw, Maryland doesn't have the death penalty anymore, but he better not ever see daylight again." Milo stated with anger.

Valentina felt her heart break all over again, the weight of their loss heavy on her shoulders. They weren't saying shit she could use. And she needed someone to say the right thing. It would've been her aunt Jessie, but she was home sick with flu-like symptoms.

Overcome with physical and emotional pain, she leaned her head back against the seat, her eyes closed as she tried to process her reality.

"I feel like this all my fault." Valentina continued. "Had I not told RoRo's boss...he would be..."

"No, fuck that shit!" Milo yelled. "That nigga was out of pocket before you met him, and you did what you had to do. Because if you think he wouldn't blackmail them every time he got broke, you crazy. You too for that matter."

Larisa looked back at her through the rearview mirror, "Valentina, you know that nigga was dealing with his own demons, there was nothing you could have done."

Valentina shook her head, "I know you're right, but it doesn't change how I feel. And I gotta live with it for the rest of my life."

"Nah, fuck this shit. That shit's worse than cancer." Larisa pulled over and turned to face her. "Listen, you not about to be living on guilt." She paused. "Now we all loved Nevin, and we all wish we could have done more to help him, but it's not your fault. It's none of our fault. And the last thing I'm gonna let you do is kill yourself slowly because of this shit."

"Are you sure?" She trembled. "That it's not my fault? What about Ms. Alexander. Because technically, I still owe for that."

Larisa wasn't supposed to know but Valentina knew she did. She was Milo's girl now, and there was nothing stronger than pillow talk.

Larisa looked at him.

"I swear to God it's not on you." Milo said. "Let it go, before guilt comes back for more."

From where they were, they hugged each other awkwardly. It felt like forever until finally Larisa started the car again, "Let's get the fuck out of here and get you home."

They drove in silence for a while longer, each lost in their own thoughts and memories of Nevin.

As they pulled up to Valentina's new apartment, in a safe enough community in the county, she was reminded that her luxurious lifestyle was over.

She didn't care.

"I love y'all niggas," Valentina said.

"Love you too," Larisa and Milo said in unison, their voices heavy with emotion.

They hugged once more, knowing that they would always carry Nevin in their hearts.

She eased away from the car and went into her building. The cream walls smelled like fresh paint which she liked.

Keys in hand, she entered her modest one-bedroom apartment, taking in the simple design. The floors creaked beneath her feet as she made her way to the kitchen, where she could see the wooden cabinets lining the walls. She couldn't help but feel a sense of warmth in the space, despite its lack of frills.

Turning her head to the right, boxes lined the floor. And when she trudged around the apartment, she could hear rap music faintly coming from the streets outside her windows. It was a familiar sound, one that she would have to become accustomed to.

Slowly Valentina made her way back to the living room and lifted a window to allow fresh air inside. When she closed it back, she noticed the latch didn't lock. She was slightly concerned, since if someone stood on a milk crate they could get inside with no problem, but she had intentions on telling management later.

Sitting in a metal chair, the only furniture in her crib, she took a deep breath. She let out a sigh of contentment as she leaned back into the wall and closed her eyes, feeling at peace in the simplicity of the space. This was her new sanctuary, where she could escape the chaos of the city and just be...well...regular.

It may not have been the most luxurious crib in the world, but she couldn't wait to make more memories and truly call it home.

"I miss you, Nevin. I'm gonna make you proud."

EPILOGUE
SIX MONTHS LATER

Valentina sat nervously in the studio, fidgeting with her hands as she waited for her segment to begin on the podcast, An *Ugly Girl's Diary*.

Unlike in the past, this time she was a guest, and she was mad nervous.

Besides, she was fangirling hard!

Courtney was prettier than she imagined, and Valentina couldn't believe that she ever considered herself an ugly woman. Light brown skin, hazel eyes and the strawberry patch tattoo on her shoulder blade was life. "Are you okay?" Courtney asked after she was mic'd up. "Want anything to drink?"

"Uh...I..."

"Are you thirsty?" Courtney giggled.

"No...I'm just nervous."

"Don't worry, you'll be great." As the host, Courtney took a few moments to introduce her while Valentina took a deep breath and tried to steady her nerves. "So, Valentina, welcome to the show," Courtney said with a warm smile. "I understand you a superfan."

"You don't even know the half."

Courtney smiled. "Well we're so excited to have you here to share your story with our listeners."

Valentina nodded, her throat feeling tight with emotion. "Thank you for having me," she managed to choke out.

"So, can you tell us a little bit about what you want to share with our audience today?" Courtney prompted.

Valentina breathed deeply again. "My story is...well...I want to talk about revenge," she said, her voice shaking slightly. "And how it took everything from me, including my brother."

Courtney's expression grew serious. "That sounds like a very powerful and emotional story. Are you sure you'll be able to do this?"

Silence.

"Valentina. Are you sure?"

"Uh...yeah."

"Well can you tell us more about what happened?"

Valentina nodded, her eyes filling with tears. "It all started with a cell phone," she began, her voice breaking."

"I'm confused."

"I found a phone in my house, after a party, and thought the messages in it were about me." She looked down and up again. "I guess there's something to be said by everything ain't about you. But by the time I learned this, it was too late."

As Valentina spoke, Courtney listened intently, nodding along, and offering words of encouragement. Things were going well. And as time passed, Valentina's voice broke as she spoke of her brother, the things she did for paper and the new world she was grateful for that was surrounded in peace.

Tears streamed down her face as she continued to release her soul. "I just want people to know that revenge is not worth it. It destroyed my life and my family. And I will never forget the cost of my actions."

Courtney appreciated the tale, but she begged to differ. "Well, maybe in your situation it was a bad move. But I'm here to tell you, revenge, served right, is still sweet."

LATER THAT NIGHT

Courtney sat on the sofa, surrounded by the familiar sights, and sounds of her home. The TV was on, the blue light flickered in the dark room, and she was at peace. The smell of cooking from earlier still lingered in the air, a comforting aroma that filled her nostrils because her meal was good. Besides, at one point she was imprisoned for accidentally killing her roommate who took her child.

So she still appreciated being free.

She sighed, relishing the quiet moment after a long day of hosting her hit podcast, Valentina, her recent guest, had her questioning the purpose of the show but at the same time she was about revenge.

She was so much about it that she had...well...lost peace.

When her phone rang, she answered. "Hello."

"Hey...it's me."

"You don't have to say it's me, Adrienne. I know my studio engineer's voice when I hear it." She giggled.

"Is your son near you?" Her voice was serious.

"No...he's asleep. To be thirteen he sleeps all damn day. What's up?"

"It's about your guest...Valentina."

She sat up straight. "What about her?"

"She was burned in her apartment tonight."

"What...is she...is she alive?"

"First let me say yes. And I know you don't like me mingling with the guests, but I visited and she's in ICU with burns over most of her body. They caught the girl who was responsible on camera. It was somebody named Pumpkin."

"Are you...are you serious?"

"Yeah, her boyfriend...I think his name is Jacob is taking care of her though. He seems to care a lot so at least she has that."

"But I thought she said he left her on our show."

"I know when a nigga cares and he gives a fuck. Trust me. Saw it with my eyes. And you won't believe it, but I think she looked...relieved. I could be wrong, but I think she'll be okay."

Maybe revenge wasn't for everyone after all.

The phone dropped from her hand and fell on the sofa just as a knock startled her from her thoughts. Slowly she rose from the couch, her heart racing, and made her way to the door.

When she opened it wide, her brother Posea, stood on the other side, his expression tense.

"Hey, what is it?" She asked, fear creeping into her soul. Something was up. She could tell in his eyes. "Dinner is tomorrow."

Her brother's words were like a punch to the gut. "He's getting out, Courtney. The nigga Tye getting out of prison on a technicality."

"What the fuck?"

"They calling him the Technicality King, because it'll be the second time."

Courtney felt a cold sweat break out on her forehead. She worked so hard to keep the memories of her past locked away, to build a new life for her son and to help people on her show get at niggas who deserved it. And now, it seemed like all of that was about to come to a screeching halt.

"How did this happen?" She whispered, her voice barely audible.

"Another podcast ran by some dudes," her brother replied. "They saying niggas is innocent and getting hemmed up on account of your show. They found some loopholes, raised some money and it worked. He free."

"Do you have eyes on him?"

"Yeah...but I think he wants to see him."

"Who?"

"His son."

288

Courtney walked away and sank into the couch, her head in her hands. The room was silent except for the sound of the TV, a haunting background noise to the chaos in her mind.

Then she felt her brother's hand on her shoulder, and she looked up into his eyes. Filled with determination and strength he said, "You got family now, Courtney. And we'll keep you safe. I won't let shit happen to you or nephew. Fuck that nigga."

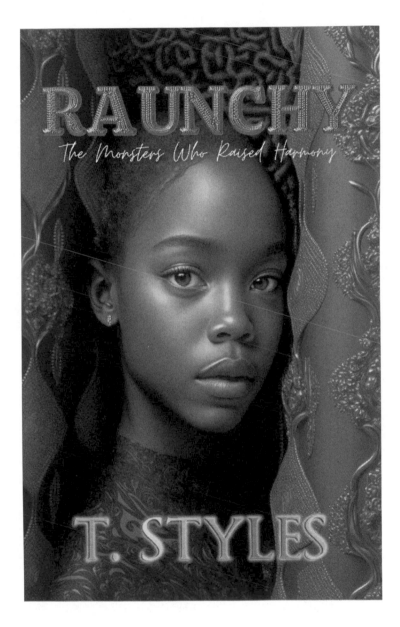

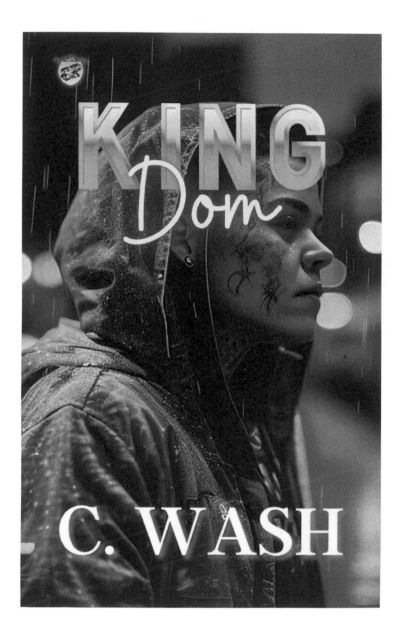

The Cartel Publications Order Form

www.thecartelpublications.com

Inmates **ONLY** receive novels for $12.00 per book **PLUS** shipping fee **PER BOOK.**

(Mail Order **MUST** come from inmate directly to receive discount)

Shyt List 1	_____	$15.00
Shyt List 2	_____	$15.00
Shyt List 3	_____	$15.00
Shyt List 4	_____	$15.00
Shyt List 5	_____	$15.00
Shyt List 6	_____	$15.00
Pitbulls In A Skirt	_____	$15.00
Pitbulls In A Skirt 2	_____	$15.00
Pitbulls In A Skirt 3	_____	$15.00
Pitbulls In A Skirt 4	_____	$15.00
Pitbulls In A Skirt 5	_____	$15.00
Victoria's Secret	_____	$15.00
Poison 1	_____	$15.00
Poison 2	_____	$15.00
Hell Razor Honeys	_____	$15.00
Hell Razor Honeys 2	_____	$15.00
A Hustler's Son	_____	$15.00
A Hustler's Son 2	_____	$15.00
Black and Ugly	_____	$15.00
Black and Ugly As Ever	_____	$15.00
Ms Wayne & The Queens of DC **(LGBTQ)**	_____	$15.00
Black And The Ugliest	_____	$15.00
Year Of The Crackmom	_____	$15.00
Deadheads	_____	$15.00
The Face That Launched A Thousand Bullets	_____	$15.00
The Unusual Suspects	_____	$15.00
Paid In Blood	_____	$15.00
Raunchy	_____	$15.00
Raunchy 2	_____	$15.00
Raunchy 3	_____	$15.00
Mad Maxxx (4th Book Raunchy Series)	_____	$15.00
Quita's Dayscare Center	_____	$15.00
Quita's Dayscare Center 2	_____	$15.00
Pretty Kings	_____	$15.00
Pretty Kings 2	_____	$15.00
Pretty Kings 3	_____	$15.00
Pretty Kings 4	_____	$15.00
Silence Of The Nine	_____	$15.00
Silence Of The Nine 2	_____	$15.00
Silence Of The Nine 3	_____	$15.00
Prison Throne	_____	$15.00

Drunk & Hot Girls	$15.00
Hersband Material **(LGBTQ)** _	$15.00
The End: How To Write A	$15.00
Bestselling Novel In 30 Days (Non-Fiction Guide)	
Upscale Kittens	$15.00
Wake & Bake Boys	$15.00
Young & Dumb	$15.00
Young & Dumb 2: Vyce's Getback	$15.00
Tranny 911 **(LGBTQ)**	$15.00
Tranny 911: Dixie's Rise **(LGBTQ)**	$15.00
First Comes Love, Then Comes Murder	$15.00
Luxury Tax	$15.00
The Lying King	$15.00
Crazy Kind Of Love	$15.00
Goon	$15.00
And They Call Me God	$15.00
The Ungrateful Bastards	$15.00
Lipstick Dom **(LGBTQ)**	$15.00
A School of Dolls **(LGBTQ)**	$15.00
Hoetic Justice	$15.00
KALI: Raunchy Relived	$15.00
(5th Book in Raunchy Series)	
Skeezers	$15.00
Skeezers 2	$15.00
You Kissed Me, Now I Own You	$15.00
Nefarious	$15.00
Redbone 3: The Rise of The Fold	$15.00
The Fold (4th Redbone Book)	$15.00
Clown Niggas	$15.00
The One You Shouldn't Trust	$15.00
The WHORE The Wind	
Blew My Way	$15.00
She Brings The Worst Kind	$15.00
The House That Crack Built	$15.00
The House That Crack Built 2	15.00
The House That Crack Built 3	$15.00
The House That Crack Built 4	$15.00
Level Up **(LGBTQ)**	$15.00
Villains: It's Savage Season	$15.00
Gay For My Bae	$15.00
War	$15.00
War 2: All Hell Breaks Loose	$15.00
War 3: The Land Of The Lou's	$15.00
War 4: Skull Island	$15.00
War 5: Karma	$15.00
War 6: Envy	$15.00
War 7: Pink Cotton	$15.00
Madjesty vs. Jayden (Novella)	$8.99
You Left Me No Choice	$15.00
Truce – A War Saga (War 8)	$15.00
Ask The Streets For Mercy	$15.00
Truce 2 (War 9)	$15.00
An Ace and Walid Very, Very Bad Christmas (War 10)	$15.00
Truce 3 – The Sins of The Fathers (War 11)	$15.00
Truce 4: The Finale (War 12)	$15.00
Treason	$20.00
Treason 2	$20.00
Hersband Material 2 **(LGBTQ)**	$15.00
The Gods Of Everything Else (War 13)	$15.00
The Gods Of Everything Else 2 (War 14)	$15.00
Treason 3	$15.99
An Ugly Girl's Diary	$15.99

The Gods Of Everything Else 3 (War 15) _____ $15.99
An Ugly Girl's Diary 2 _____ $19.99

(**Redbone 1** & **2** are **NOT** Cartel Publications novels and if **ordered** the cost is **FULL** price of $16.00 **each plus shipping**. **No Exceptions**.)

Please add **$7.00** for shipping and handling fees for up to **(2) BOOKS PER ORDER**. (INMATES INCLUDED) (See next page for details)

The Cartel Publications * P.O. BOX 486 OWINGS MILLS MD 21117

Name: _____

Address: _____

City/State: _____

Contact/Email: _____

Please allow 10-15 BUSINESS days Before shipping.

PLEASE NOTE DUE TO COVID-19 SOME ORDERS MAY TAKE UP TO 3 WEEKS OR LONGER BEFORE THEY SHIP

The Cartel Publications is NOT responsible for Prison Orders rejected!

**NO RETURNS and NO REFUNDS
NO PERSONAL CHECKS ACCEPTED
STAMPS NO LONGER ACCEPTED**

294

Made in the USA
Middletown, DE
18 February 2023